petr July 2018

MW01519453

SAM CRESCENT

EVERNIGHT PUBLISHING ®

www.evernightpublishing.com

Copyright© 2017

Sam Crescent

Editor: Karyn White

Cover Artist: Sour Cherry Designs

Jacket Design: Jay Aheer

ISBN: 978-1-77339-207-3

SAM CRESCENT

BESTSELLING BBW ROMANCE
SPICY ROMANCE FOR REAL WOMEN

EASY

Trojans MC, 7

Sam Crescent

Copyright © 2017

Prologue

"We can turn back," Duke said.

"No, we can't turn back. We have to do what we can to protect the club, right?" Holly said.

Duke stared at his woman, holding her hand. He knew she was going through a lot of shit right now. More shit than he could even begin to imagine. There was a life that she had never gotten to know, and would never know. Lies upon lies that had not only hurt the club but her as well. He hated that she was never going to get that time back with her real father. Even if the bastard was a piece of shit, but then again, at least she wouldn't have to deal with the trauma if he was a piece of shit.

"This is all just so surreal to me right now, Duke. I don't … nothing makes sense anymore. My life, my dad, everything. I've been living with a guy I thought was my father, and he's not. I've lived a total lie, and what makes it worse, Mom and Russ haven't always been happy. They've been so miserable with each other. Why do it? Why risk it? Maybe it doesn't matter. I doubt they even know why they did."

"Do you think they stayed together because of the

risk with Abelli?" he asked.

"I don't know. All I know for certain right now is this could go to complete crap in a second. We're protecting Maya, and I think she's like my half-sister. My real father is the kind of man that doesn't mind ordering the rape and torture of his own daughter, and she's just a kid, Duke. Younger than Matthew, and he's a baby as well."

"Matthew would argue that."

"I'm terrified, Duke. I'm scared that the club will be torn apart, and I'll have to watch innocent people die. Our friends, our family. I can't live with that. I won't."

"I'm going to do everything in my power to protect you, Holly. You, our family, our club, and the Trojans belong to us. We're the ones that run it, together. I'll never go down without fighting."

She nodded, and he saw the tears in her eyes, the fear. He hated that she felt any kind of fear.

"Let's do this."

Climbing out of his car, he rounded the vehicle, and helped Holly out.

Entering the restaurant, Duke noted several waiters who were in fact bodyguards. This was the most logical way of entering Abelli territory. They were lucky that they hadn't been shot on sight, and he was sure the only reason they hadn't been was because of Abelli wanting to know his daughter. The one that was taken from him.

"Over here," a rough voice said.

Putting a hand on Holly's back, Duke made sure to guard her, making sure no one had a shot at his wife. He would die protecting her, and Pike knew if anything happened to him, he was to take care of Holly. The club would avenge him.

They were just a simple MC. They played hard,

fucked hard, but when it came to their women, and their club, they were fucking savages. No one stole from them. No one hurt who they cared about and got away with it.

"Abelli?" he asked, taking a seat after Holly.

The man's face was shrouded in darkness. Duke didn't like not being able to see his opponent.

"It is I," he said, leaning forward.

Holly let out a gasp, and Duke wasn't feeling all that good either. The man's face was something out of a horror movie, gashes and burn marks. There was nothing remotely human looking about him, apart from his eyes.

"Does it shock you?" Abelli asked.

"You look like a nightmare," Duke said, being honest.

Abelli burst out laughing. "You'd think that this face would stop me being popular with the ladies, but I've got enough money that I can make whores lick my face as I ride their pussies."

"Ew," Holly said.

"I'd appreciate it if you don't talk like that in front of my girl."

"So this is my daughter." Abelli lit a cigarette with his gaze focused on Holly. "You're pretty."

"Thank you," she said.

"Wow, you've also got manners. You sure Russ has been pretending to be your father? That fucker didn't have a polite bone in his body when I knew him."

"He let you live, didn't he?" she asked. "I'd say that is pretty polite."

"I'm a human monster. I'm like a superhero with no great abilities. I'm used for one thing, and one thing only. I'm the monster, the bogeyman that people are afraid of. The only difference is I am fucking real," Abelli said. "Regardless of who or what I am, are you happy, Holly?"

Duke didn't take his gaze away from Abelli. He didn't trust the fucker. Over the years his instincts hadn't let him down, and right now, he didn't trust anything this man said or did.

"I don't know if this is supposed to be a trick question or not."

"I want to know the truth about you. Are you happy?"

"Yeah, I am. I'm a mother," she said. "Erm, I, er, I don't … my memories are vague, and I didn't remember you until recently."

"Your mother decided to shack up with a Trojan, and I can't say that I blame her to a point. I wasn't exactly the model husband. I fucked every woman that walked in my path, and I loved it. She was a dutiful wife until Russ came along and started to fill her head with shit. Couldn't get to them though. One thing Trojans have, it's a reputation that no one wants to mess with, not even me."

Duke held onto Holly's hand as she squeezed it tightly. Russ had built the Trojans up, and Duke had to wonder if he did it right after Anton, or even just before. The Abelli hadn't come out for revenge. Just by looking at him, Duke knew he had to have been in some serious need of recovery. The scars on Anton's face, that wasn't a week of healing. No, the scars on his face must have taken months. Enough time to give the Trojans a reputation that rivaled most.

"You've got a lot of brothers and sister. Bastards, and some of them hate me probably as much as Maya does." Duke didn't make a move, but Holly did. "Ah, I knew you had her in your care. I couldn't give a shit what she told the lawyer friend or cop friend of hers. She's not the only one speaking out against us. She won't be the first, and she won't be the last. What makes it interesting is that she's now with the same man that did this to my face, and took my woman and kid."

"You knew where I was this whole time?" Holly asked.

"Yes, of course. The truth is I couldn't give a shit about Sheila or Russ, or you, and it seems that the Trojans have a reputation that goes far beyond family loyalty."

"You're saying that your own family wouldn't exact revenge?" Duke asked.

"Let's just say I'm not the most well-liked. Anyway, you're here because you have something of mine, and as it is, my family wants to silence Maya. I'll offer you a trade. I'll take Russ or Sheila, and you can keep Maya. Make sure she stays quiet, and that lawyer friend of yours, he'll live as well. If not, I'll destroy the town of Vale Valley, and every single person within it personally."

"You expect me to give you my mother or my father?" Holly asked.

"Or I will make sure Matthew doesn't live to see his place within the Trojans. Drake and Bell, I will kill them as well. The choice is yours, and I think all things considered, I've been reasonable."

Chapter One

"You're an embarrassment to this family. You think we don't know where you are?" her father asked.

Eliza listened to her father rant and rave, and she hadn't even gotten the chance to say hello yet.

"Darcy is on his way down there. He's going to sort this out, and then there will be no more crap anymore."

She rolled her eyes, and then snorted. Darcy against Brass, there was no competition. Brass would crush Darcy like a bug. The man her parents wanted her to marry was in fact gay, and had even told her so. The marriage was just a ruse to make sure he could continue his lifestyle, all the time she was looking like the doting wife. Darcy didn't even expect her to find a man for herself. He even told her that she was too fat and ugly to have a man who wanted her.

Well, not only did she have a man that wanted her, he was damn good as well.

"That's good to know, Dad. Really, it was great listening to you again," she said. For some strange reason she really didn't give a shit about what he had to say. It was the first time in her life that she really didn't care about her father, his opinions, or even trying to impress him. He wanted her to give up her whole life for a guy he'd picked out, who was in fact cruel, mean, and hurtful. "I've got to go now. Oh, if Darcy thinks he can come and get me, tell him that's okay, but I'm seeing someone, so he can kiss my fat, ugly ass."

She hung up the phone, and took a deep breath to smile. She could smile.

The sound of clapping hands made her jump, and as she spun around, she saw Brass was standing in the doorway.

"I didn't know you were there," she said.

"This is my apartment, babe. I went to get you coffee. Fat, ugly ass? Do I need to spank you for that shit?"

She shook her head. "No, not at all. I told you about Darcy, my supposed husband to be?"

"Yeah, you may have mentioned him when I was balls deep inside your sweet pussy." He handed her a steaming cup of takeout coffee. The bag he had in his other hand smelled delicious. Brass, last name and even first name unknown, but she didn't care. She was just basking in the fun with him. Never had she been able to be herself, and yet, Brass demanded it.

"Well it's what he told me. He's gay. Has a guy who he actually sleeps with. It kind of sucks really, to be honest."

"Wait, wait, wait. You're telling me that the guy your father wants you to marry likes dudes? He takes dick?"

"I guess he is. He also gives it." She had walked into his office when he had been giving it to his boyfriend. It had been a real eye opener. "Do you have a problem with that?"

"I don't give a shit about a guy's preference. Personally, I love a good pair of tits, a nice tight pussy, and with you, I actually like talking to you."

"Wow, thank you." She chuckled. She had stayed in Vale Valley a couple of weeks, and had found that Brass wasn't being mean, or blunt. This was simply who he was. There was no underlying motive. He loved to fuck, ride his bike, and party. The partying wasn't really her scene, and apart from going to see Knuckles and Beth's wedding, she hadn't participated in any of the parties. She wasn't going to give Brass a reason to send her on her merry way. She was known for being a stick in the mud, and right now, she wanted to enjoy the small freedom she had been given.

There would come a time she had to give up, but until then, she was going to try to keep this happiness for some time.

"It's not that, babe, you know it. I just—he told you that you were fat and ugly."

"Yes. His demands in marrying me were that I'm to give the show of loyal, forgiving wife, and even though he can have a man of his own, I'm not allowed any." She shrugged. "I guess this is what you call a little rebellion. Sounds great, huh?"

Brass put down the coffee and bag of food down. Her stomach chose that moment to growl. "You're hurt?"

"No, I'm not hurt." She blew out a breath. "Okay, maybe I am. Growing up I always wanted to have the kind of marriage you read about in books or see in the movies." She felt the tears starting to build, and she took a breath. Years of keeping them at bay, the training wasn't forgotten, and she wasn't about to spill them over. She stared down at her hands. "It's silly."

"It's not silly." He placed a finger beneath her chin and tilted her head back. "Never believe that something like that can be silly. Wanting that kind of shit, it's natural."

"Did you?"

"No. I didn't want to be. My folks were constantly at each other's throats," he said.

"My parents pretended the other didn't exist. I'm not trying to get pity or anything. It's just the way it is." She pressed her hands against his chest, not to push him away, just because she wanted to touch him.

"You're not okay, are you, baby?"

"I am. It's just ... talking with my dad always makes me feel like I failed. Like I fucked up big time."

She tried not to care what he thought, but the truth was, she did. She cared a lot. "I can't even marry the right man."

Brass stroked her cheek, and she stared into his eyes, finding comfort in his stare. He was big, so powerful. She loved it when his muscular, inked arms surrounded her. The way he groaned each time his cock plunged inside her as if he couldn't hold in the pleasure.

"You're thinking dirty thoughts right now, aren't you?"

"A little bit."

He slammed his lips down on hers, and she wrapped her arms around his neck, forgetting about the coffee, and everything else. His hands were on her back, pushing up her sweater, and flicking the catch of her bra. She should care that he knew how to do that, and with such ease, and yet she didn't.

His experience was her gain. Brass shoved her against the wall, and gathered up her skirt, and tearing away her panties. "What have I told you about wearing these?" he asked.

"Not to, unless it's that time of the month."

"Nothing has changed." He released her long enough to tear open a condom, and then his hands were on her ass, lifting her up. "Oh fuck! Tight, so fucking tight," he said, filling her with his cock.

He was so long and thick. Each thrust filled her to the brim and then some more.

"Oh, God," she said, gripping onto his shoulders as he began to thrust inside her. The hold he had on her ass would leave a bruise. She didn't mind. In the past couple of weeks her body was covered in Brass shaped marks. Good bruises from some hard fucking, and boy, did she love fucking him.

"That's right, baby. You're not marrying the right

man because there is no other man out there that can give you what you need." One of his hands left her ass, and he tore her skirt away. "Watch us, Eliza. Watch my cock fill your pussy."

She looked down, seeing his cock pull out and thrust forward. The condom was covered with her cream. She was so damn aroused, and already she was addicted to his cock. Nothing else would do for her.

"You're mine, Eliza. You don't want the prim fucking life of the rich. You want to be with a man who knows how to take care of you. Who knows how to get you so fucking dirty that you don't ever want to be clean. I can give that to you. Your body craves me."

Eliza leaned forward, sliding her tongue against his pulse as she reached between them, and started to tease her clit. Stroking over the bud, she felt the beginnings of her orgasm. Brass held her ass once again, and started to thrust up, harder, bumping her hand as they fucked against the wall.

She screamed his name as her orgasm caught her and threw her into that zone where she didn't give a fuck about anything, only the pleasure that Brass could give her. He had taken her to this point of pleasure that she never wanted to leave Vale Valley, or him.

Brass came, and even through the condom and her own orgasm, she felt the pulses of his cock, and she wished there was no condom between them. She would love to just let loose and give into the need that he awakened inside her.

Together they sank down to the floor, and she pushed her hair out of her face and smiled down at him. Brass moved them so that his cock was still inside her, and she straddled his hips.

"You're going to kill me."

She laughed. "You're the one that started this."

She ran her fingers through his hair and played with a few strands at his neck. There was nothing clean-cut about him, and she loved that.

"You don't have to think about husbands or shit like that."

"I should stay here forever?" she asked.

"Yeah, if that's what you want," he said.

They had started fucking a few weeks ago when her car had finally been fixed. Once again, she stared into his eyes, and wondered if she could do it. Could she stay? He wasn't on his knees begging her, or declaring love for her.

There was no way she was ever going to expect something like that. Declarations of love never happened to her, and Eliza was under no illusions about what this was. She was an easy fuck.

The Trojans were notorious around these parts, and she was simply a girl in a long line of them. The only difference was she was the only sleeping with one of them.

"I'm hungry," she said, pulling off his cock.

What had started out as fun was fast starting to take its toll. She didn't know what hurt more, the thought of staying and watching him with other women, or leaving.

It was a decision she had to make.

****

Brass stared at the car in front of him, and he really didn't give a shit if it rode again. He was pissed off, and angry, which was the fucking same thing, but it didn't.

"You okay?" Knuckles asked.

"Fine!" He snapped the word out.

"This have something to do with that piece of ass you've been screwing?" Pie asked, sitting on one of the bonnets of the car, eating a fucking hand pie.

"Fuck off. I'm not about to talk about pussy shit." Brass rubbed his hands on the cloth and glared at the car.

"Just so you know, Duke finished that car yesterday. You've been standing there looking at it for over an hour," Knuckles said, patting his arm. "We're just waiting for it to be collected."

"Fuck! Why the fuck am I here?" Brass asked.

"You're not scheduled to work here today. You're supposed to be helping Landon with the beer run," Pie said. "You've not been with it. Does that posh woman you've been fucking got a memory loss pussy or something?"

Brass gritted his teeth and threw his cloth against the hood of the car. "Fuck."

"You keep saying that, but we're all curious. You used to be with it, Brass," Knuckles said.

"Look, it's nothing okay? I'm fine. I'm just dealing with the same old shit is all." He wasn't dealing with anything. The truth was, he was in love with his posh, wealthy woman, and he didn't have a fucking clue how to handle that.

"I'm heading out for my honeymoon in a couple of weeks. I promised Duke that I'd stick around after getting married, but then Beth and I, we're going to celebrate. Shit is about to go down. We all know it, and I need you to know that you can still reach out to me. Got it?" Knuckles said.

"You do know that a honeymoon has always been a quiet time for your woman, Knuckles. No one will call you. It's our club way," Brass said. "Don't worry. We can all handle it. I don't see anything getting past Pike and Duke."

"Yeah, well, I've put off this honeymoon gig for long enough. Beth deserves romance, and all that shit."

EASY

Brass laughed. "You love giving her that shit, so don't even go pretending to us that you're not looking forward to your woman, alone on a nice exotic beach away from prying eyes, and all that bull."

"I do, I just … this shit with Abelli, you can't deny it's crazy."

Brass thought about that young girl, Maya, and they had to remember her name was Winter. "Speaking of Winter, how is Landon holding up?" Brass asked.

"He's doing good. Taking Winter around, protecting her and shit. It's all good," Pie said.

"Are we going to have to worry about how good that is?" Knuckles asked. "The girl has only just turned sixteen."

"No, God, ugh, no. Landon is treating her like a sister. I don't think it has even registered on his brain that she's one of those females he can fuck or anything," Pie said. "She's the same as Zoe."

Zoe was Raoul's woman, and an old lady. No one messed with a club lady. Club whores, yes.

Brass wondered if Eliza would be able to hack the club lady lifestyle. Just the thought of her in his leather jacket made him hard as rock. Of course she wouldn't be wearing anything else, and he was more than okay with that.

Some men liked women on the slender side where their bones were practically peeking through their skin. Him, he liked his woman with some meat on her bones so he could hold onto her as he fucked her hard, claiming her.

"You got that dreamy look on your face," Knuckles said.

"Fuck off. I'm out of here." Brass left the garage and climbed on his bike, taking him back toward the clubhouse. The moment he parked up he saw Matthew

17

was sitting on the wall, smoking a cigarette, and typing on his damn cell phone. "I thought you were in college?"

"I am. Dad wants me to work from home for a few weeks. He said it's important, and so I'm here."

"Holly will kick your ass if she finds you smoking."

"I know. It's part of her charm, don't you think?" Matthew asked, laughing.

"You're a crazy assed fucker." He wouldn't have Holly kicking his ass for anything. That woman was deadly, and besides, she had a far worse trick up her sleeve. She could deny them her food. Holly and Mary had a food blog going, and they practiced their recipes on the whole club. They were true goddesses of the kitchen, and Brass for one fucking adored them, and their food. Without them, they would be back to fast food and ready meals. He wasn't down with that.

He wouldn't admit it, but if they asked him to get down on one knee and worship them, he'd gladly do it.

"Just go toward the shouting. It's not hard to miss at all!" Matthew yelled toward him.

The instant he hit the doorway of the club, he heard the arguing. It was pretty hard to ignore.

"Are you fucking stupid or something?" Russ asked.

Wow, this was not a good day.

Still, he was a Trojan, and he wasn't a pussy, so he pushed his way through, and paused as he saw a standoff in the main clubroom. Duke and Russ were facing each other, and it looked like they were ready to come to blows.

Not good.

"Do you think I wanted to deal with this shit? This is the kind of shit someone deals with when they hand over the fucking gavel, Russ. Not years later when

I've got to fucking act!"

"I did what I thought was right. You taking in that whore, you should have left her behind," Russ said.

"I can't believe you're speaking like that," Holly said. "Winter was in need."

"You know what? Cut the crap. We don't need to give her a fake fucking name. Her name is Maya Abelli. He already knows we have her. We may as well own the fucking title," Russ said.

Brass folded his arms and leaned against the wall. Russ was the previous Prez of the Trojans MC. He'd handed the gavel over to Duke, who had been leading them for nearly ten years now. Duke was also the husband to Holly, Russ's daughter. Only now, it had come to light that Russ wasn't her father at all. In fact he'd stolen Holly with her mother Sheila away from a mafia guy known as Abelli.

Shit was just getting worse and worse.

"You got a problem with me, Russ?" Duke asked.

"Yeah, I do. You're going to put all of us in danger, and you don't even give a shit."

"Enough," Sheila said, speaking up. "We cannot undo the past. We all fucked up! We can't change what we did. Now, tell us what we can do to fix it."

Brass watched as Duke looked toward Holly. "He wants either you or Russ."

Silence fell on the room, and Brass couldn't quite comprehend what he had just heard.

"Seriously?" Russ asked.

"Yeah, I'm being fucking serious right now," Duke said. "Either I give him one of you, or shit comes to the club."

"You can't do that."

"I have no intention of doing that," Duke said. "Right now, I've not got a lot of choice."

"He was never the most stable, Duke. He will try to ruin you, the club, everything," Sheila said.

"Then I'll do everything in my power to make sure that doesn't happen."

There was silence once again, and Brass chose that moment to leave the clubhouse. Shit was about to go down, and it was about to get ugly real fucking fast.

Chapter Two

Eliza frowned at her account, and was so pissed off she couldn't even think straight right now. All of her money was gone. Technically, it was her father's money, but still. He had paid her every single month because he didn't want her to work, and now this shit.

Taking her card, she placed it in her purse and spun around, taking a deep breath.

"You okay?" a woman said.

She opened her eyes, which she had closed, to see a beautiful curvy woman with brown hair and eyes. Also, she was vaguely familiar. "Martha, Matilda, no, Mary, right," Eliza said.

"Yeah, that's me. I'm Pike's old lady. I usually wear his jacket, but right now, I'm not really in a leather mood." For some strange reason Mary patted her stomach with a smile on her lips. "You're Eliza right? The girl that Brass can't seem to get enough of."

"Er, yeah, that is me." Was she Brass's girl, or just the girl that he was fucking right now?

Enough.

"Are you okay? You look a little ... stressed."

Eliza glanced down seeing the young girl staring back up at her.

"Oh, this is Starlight. Sweetie, this is Eliza. She's Brass's special friend."

"I want to be someone's special friend, Mommy."

"Yeah, you will one day." Mary looked back at her and shook her head. "Not that kind though. I've got to drop Starlight off at school, and then we can go and have some breakfast if you would like."

"Oh, that is really nice."

"But? Do you have other plans?" Mary asked.

"No. I don't. I'd love to have breakfast with you."

She walked alongside Mary and her daughter listening to their conversation, which was strange. They were talking about a chocolate cupcake recipe, and Mary was asking all kind of questions to her little girl. By the time they were finished, Eliza stood outside of the school gate watching as Mary hugged her daughter, kissed her, and promised to make lots of cupcakes with her later on.

"Hey, sorry if we bore you. Food is our thing, and also mine and Holly, and Leanna's."

"It was different. Are you a chef?"

"A food blogger. Holly and I set it up, and it has become a full-time deal. We have to create, test, and test some more all different and new recipes. We also do book testers as well. Some of the stuff we do at the club, at our homes, and stuff. Do you cook?"

Eliza found herself nodding. "I do cook. I enjoy it. It's not something I was allowed to do all the time." Her father had told her only common people cooked for themselves, and she was not a common person. She hated her father.

"Wow, who kept control of you?" Mary asked.

"Oh, my dad. He liked to make sure everyone knew he was in charge, and he was."

"Sounds like a total asshole to me."

"He is."

"He's still alive?"

"Yeah, he just, erm, he paid me to not work if that makes sense, and I just went to withdraw some money, and he's cleared it."

"He's emptied your account?" When Eliza nodded, Mary asked, "Is that even legal?"

"Probably. It is his money. I didn't do anything." She wasn't allowed to do anything. About three years ago she'd started writing, short stories and novellas. She loved the release of all of her thoughts and fantasies. One day she decided to be rebellious and submit them. She did, and after a great deal of rejection, there was one company who wanted her. Of course, she agreed, and her sense of freedom lasted four months.

Her father found out, terminated everything, and put the entire company out of business. Any future she hoped to have always died. For the first time in Vale Valley, she had felt free … far away from his reach. Now he was going to make life difficult for her.

"Come on. You need my homemade mocha, and you need it now." They were standing outside a large house.

"This is your home?"

"Yep. We also live at the clubhouse whenever Pike needs us to, but this is our home. It has a killer kitchen inside. Come on."

Entering Mary's home she was overcome with the scent of fresh baking and cinnamon. Her mouth watered, and her stomach growled.

"So, no money, is that why you were looking ready to burst into tears by the ATM machine?"

"Yeah, I guess I was."

"Don't worry. You're not the only person seen doing that. Usually it's because someone has forgotten their number. It's no big deal." They entered a large kitchen with up to date equipment. In the corner she saw a large table set up with at least three cameras at different angles. "Pike supports my career, although he keeps complaining that he has to build a gym at home to work everything off." Mary shrugged. "I love him either way."

Eliza didn't have a clue what to say. Her parents didn't believe in love, and at times she didn't think it existed either. "Do you know of anyone who wants someone who can work hard?"

"Have you had a job before? I know it's a rude

question, but you said your father paid you not to work."

She blew out a breath. "For a few months I was an erotic author. Does that count?"

Mary chuckled. "Yeah, it does. So your father is the overbearing kind?"

"You can say that. Overbearing. Constantly making demands. It sucks. All of this sucks."

"I heard through the gossip that he's forcing you to get married. Isn't there a law about that kind of thing?" Mary asked.

"I don't know. I doubt anyone would take me seriously. Who in their right mind would give up total luxury?" Eliza ran fingers through her hair and groaned. "Darcy, he's gay, and he wants me to be the doting wife. Sitting around all day waiting for him, but the only probl—"

"Whoa, whoa, whoa, the guy they want you to spend the rest of your life with is into other guys?"

"Yeah."

"Do you get to be with other guys?"

"Nope."

"That sucks. You know what, Eliza? You came to the right place. Vale Valley may be small, but we're a good bunch. Brass is a good guy. Somewhat slow but he's a good guy."

"Slow?"

"It takes him a long time to make up his mind about something. Anyway, how about you stick around, and help me and Holly out."

"With what? You seem to have this operation down." She pointed toward the camera. "Can you show me your site?"

"Totally." A buzzer went off, and Mary held up a finger. "After you've tried my cinnamon rolls." Mary hummed as she got the rolls out of the oven, and Eliza watched in amazement as she made up a quick glaze and poured it right on top. "I love it when it soaks in, and some parts are really sweet."

With a laptop between them, a small plate of pastries, and a homemade mocha latte, they were looking at the website that Holly and Mary had created. "We were going to go with something food related, and then we decided on using our connections to the MC, and so, ta-da, 'Eat the Trojan MC Way'."

"It's catchy," Eliza said, moaning as she took a bite of the warm roll. It was so damn good.

"I know, right. We figured as all of our men try our food, it was only nice of us to give them some credit."

"It's nice." She thought about Brass, and wondered if there were times he wanted to come home to nice cooked meal, and maybe have any kids, a family or a future. "So, what do you know about Brass?"

Mary smiled. "You like him, don't you?"

"Of course I like him. I wouldn't be having sex with him if I didn't."

"Why don't you tell me what you like about him, and I can tell you if you're missing anything." Mary took a sip of her coffee.

"It's not just about the sex. It's fun, and I love it, but we talk as well. He reads a lot, which surprised me. He loves books, and watching movies. Cowboy movies are a big deal to him." Eliza smiled remembering a memory he had shared of standing in front of the television pretending to draw a weapon. He had even shown her. "He enjoys sprinkles on his vanilla ice cream, and he thinks it's a little weird that he loves such a plain flavor. I love peanut butter ice cream."

"My kind of girl."

"When I'm with Brass, I don't know, he makes

me smile, and he doesn't have to try. I can't tell you exactly what I like about him, I just know that every time my father tries to tear me away, I'm scared that I'm going to crumble and lose Brass." She slapped a hand over her mouth. "I never speak so openly to anyone, ever." Her words had been used against her one too many times.

"You don't trust easily, do you?" Mary asked.

"It's hard to trust anyone when your whole life has been about hiding from that truth." She tucked some hair behind her ear.

"Can I read some of your work?" Mary asked.

"Yeah, I've got it saved in my emails. The entire company went out of business because of my father." Eliza sighed.

"You ever thought that while you're here, you should be able to start it back up?" Mary asked.

"Start what back up?"

"The writing. Your dad's not here, and if you talk to Brass, he'll back you. I know I will."

"You've not even read any of my work. I could be total crap."

"Or you could have some faith in yourself and stop being so negative." Mary patted her arm. "You're not at home anymore, and Brass is a lot of things, but he's not cruel. He won't toss you out into the cold."

"Thank you."

"I would have you as my best friend, but Holly has the BFF award."

Eliza burst out laughing. She was just happy to have a possible path.

****

"I thought you'd never turn up," Landon said, pulling up outside of the clubhouse. "What happened to you, man?"

"Sorry, I have my head full of other shit. I

completely forgot about this." Brass stared at the loaded truck and sighed. Not only did they supply the clubhouse, but the local bar as well. Seeing as they owned the bar, and paid the locals to work there, they made sure the supplies were bought and dealt with. It was just another side business, one of many. They did illegal shit, and legal shit. "Where's your little tagalong?"

"Winter is back at my house. She's studying. I enrolled her in home school, and Zoe is helping me with her education. It fucking angers me that she hasn't gone to school in over five years. Her father pulled her out as he thought it was too much of a distraction for her." Landon shook his head. "Fucker needs killing."

Brass nodded. "Yeah, he does."

Landon paused, and looked toward him. "You know something I don't know?"

If Duke didn't want them all to know yet, Brass wasn't about to cause a problem. "I don't know shit. I'm sure Duke will let us know what we're supposed to when the time is right."

"Yeah. He will." Landon ran fingers through his hair, which he had started to grow out. "She has nightmares every single night."

"What?"

"Winter. The nights are the worst. During the day, she's like this kickass girl. Nothing will bother her, and she's so strong. I forget what she's been through. There are no long stares, or vacant looks, or fear in her eyes. She's normal. At night, it's when that fear grips her, and there's nothing I can do. I want to hold her, comfort her, but she's so fucking afraid, and in the morning, I see the guilt. She's just surviving, man. She's not living. She's trying to."

Brass had seen the evidence of what her father had made others do to her. It was sick, twisted, and there was no way a woman could handle all that. Yet, Winter seemed to take it in stride. Winter, Maya, they were the same person.

"You just got to be there for her. Take your time, and eventually she will come around."

"It's a never ending battle. A hard won one. There are times I don't even know what I'm doing." Landon sighed. "Oh well. We got to keep this shit moving, right. Onwards and upwards. That's our motto."

"I think it's more a 'step out of my way or I'll fucking kill you' kind of motto."

"Either one works. You coming or what?"

"Yep."

Brass jumped up into the truck, and headed out to do the day's work. The Trojans MC was not about sitting down on your ass all day being waited on by the club pussy, and shouted at by the old ladies. They had work to do to keep the money rolling in. Sure, they did shit that wasn't entirely legal. Drug and gun runs mostly, but it was all just for the money, the rush. Also, if they didn't do it, someone else would, and they wouldn't give a shit about who they hurt in the process. For the Trojans, they had to keep Vale Valley safe. It was where they had kids, women, their very lives, and all of them wanted it to be clean.

"So, how is it going with your sexy woman?" Landon asked.

"Great." He thought about Eliza, and it made him want to fucking groan. There was pleasure, and then there was a fucking headache. He wanted her to stay with him, but he didn't know how to actually ask her without sounding like some kind of pussy. It bothered him that there was still a guy out there who was going to marry her. This was the last fucking shit he needed.

"Trouble in paradise already?"

"Yeah, no, it's fucked up. There's a guy out there who is supposed to marry her, and I think if she leaves this place, then she'll do it." Over the past few weeks, he had seen that she had absolutely no confidence. Her father would break her down, and Brass would lose her.

"Why don't you knock her up, or better yet, why don't you ask her to stay? Would that be really hard?" Landon asked.

"Asking is for pussies." He rubbed his eyes, trying to clear his mind.

"You're an asshole. You don't think Duke, Pike, Raoul, and the others haven't done a lot of asking in their time? Just ask her to stay."

"This was supposed to be easy, Landon. Just some fun that is all I offered her." And boy, had they had fun. He had licked her pussy out until she begged him to stop. They had done everything but anal, and that was because she wasn't ready. When he was near her, he couldn't keep his hands off her.

A text buzzed on his phone, and he frowned. Glancing down he saw it was from Mary. All of the club old ladies had their numbers so it wasn't that strange to get a text from one of them.

Mary: **u heard about Eliza's asshole father!**

Brass: **Duh, yeah.**

Mary: **She's broke, Brass. He's taken her money, and I've offered her a job.**

Eliza had warned him that he would try to make her life difficult to get her to go back there. *Fuck!*

He didn't want to lose her.

Brass: **I'll be there to pick her up.**

Mary: **Do you love her?**

Brass: **I'll be there.**

"Will you drop me off at Mary's house? I've got some business to take care of."

"Sure, no problem. You know if you want to own her, you can just get us to help."

With the problems simmering between Russ and Duke, Brass didn't want to start causing trouble, or even asking for help.

"Everything will be good." A few minutes later, Landon pulled up outside of Mary's house. "You sure you're okay finishing this off for me?"

"Dude, I'm dropping shit off, and then heading to the clubhouse. I've done this as a damn Prospect. I can handle this shit."

"Fine." Brass slammed the door, and headed toward the door. There was no need to knock, so he entered Mary's house calling out. He found the two of them in the kitchen. Eliza was standing behind the camera flashing away as Mary was putting the finishing touches to whatever cake she had made.

"Ah, Brass, you're here," Mary said. "I texted him so don't think anything bad."

"Oh," Eliza said, smiling. "Hey.

"Hey." Why was it always like this between them? He didn't know what he did wrong, or even *if* he did anything wrong. *Crap.* All he wanted to do was go toward her, touch her, tell her everything was going to be okay. They had known each other on a complete physical level and had talked for hours. He had never been open with anyone else.

"Wow, the tension, people," Mary said.

"I want to talk with Eliza. Can I take her?" he asked.

"Sure. Go ahead. I've already typed my number into your phone. We'll catch up soon." Eliza nodded, grabbing her bag and jacket, following him outside.

He lived about thirty minutes away from Mary and Pike by foot. Taking hold of her hand, he locked their fingers together, trying to figure out the right words.

"Mary is nice. I like her."

"She told me that your father has emptied your bank account."

"Yeah. The money I had with me has gone, and because I'm not back, he knows I've used the money he paid me." She sighed. "He's not going to stop. All my life he has had to be in control, and I hate it. I hate feeling this way." She squeezed his hand. "I feel like I can't breathe. He's everywhere."

"He's not in Vale Valley, babe. You don't have to depend on him."

"I don't want to turn into one of those girls that use you, Brass."

He stopped, and faced her. "I want you to stay."

There, he'd said it.

"Stay?"

"Here with me. I want it to be something more than fun. I want you to rely on me, and not because I'm fucking you. I want you to rely on me because that's what we are. We rely on each other." He stroked his thumb across her hand. "I know the Trojans, and I'm not some fancy assed businessman. I'll take care of you, and you'll never have to worry about your father again."

He saw tears filled her eyes. "It has been three weeks."

"I don't give a fuck. I know that I love having you around, Eliza. If, after a few months we want to end it, then we'll end it. No pressure. I'll help you. I'm not an asshole. I won't toss you out on your ass."

She smiled. "No, you're not an asshole."

"I'm not good with words, or fancy shit. I usually know what I want, and go for it, no questions asked."

"You're doing all right, Brass. Really, you are, and I'd love to. I want to work for Mary and Holly, and there's something else I'd like to do."

"What?" he asked, already willing to do whatever it took to keep her at his side.

"When I was younger I wrote, and I got accepted for publication. Anyway my dad found out, and went completely crazy. I'd like to start writing again."

He held his hand up, and grabbed his cell phone.

"What can I do for you, Brass?" Raoul asked.

"I need you to get me a decent laptop or a computer. Actually, get me both. I want it around my place in two hours." He glanced at Eliza, seeing her mouth slightly open. "Make it three." There were a lot of things he wanted to do to that mouth. Hanging up the phone, he pulled her toward him. "Whatever dream you have, whatever you need, you come to me, and I will do everything to make sure you get it."

Before he could even demand a kiss, her lips were on his, and to Brass, everything was more than right in the world.

****

Matthew blew out a lung full of smoke, and stared across the abandoned parking lot, wondering what was going on at the club. It wasn't like his dad to pull him away from college, especially with how much he wanted him to find his own path.

Each time he did, he found himself coming back to the Trojans MC. Sure, college was great, and he loved learning, but each spare moment he thought about the Prospects at the club. He wanted to make sure that he could hack it, as otherwise he was screwed.

Three Prospects had already come and gone in a matter of weeks, not being able to handle the pressure. He never realized how many boys and men thought they wanted this life. Only the strong could hack it, and it had no room for the weak.

"You okay?"

He jumped out of his skin, and spun around to see Luna. *Fuck.* He dropped his cigarette to the floor and stubbed it out. Why did she have to be the one to find him sitting on his ass thinking? He and Luna had a lot of history. She was the girl he thought for a few weeks that he had knocked up, only to discover that she wasn't pregnant. She was a chubby girl, but he didn't see her weight. No, he loved her curves and knew what they felt like in his arms.

"Yeah, yeah, I'm okay." He'd also gone from hating the thought of being a father, to wishing she had been pregnant. He was so fucked up in the head about this girl it was unreal. "Why are you in Vale valley?"

"I had no choice but to come home."

"Oh, why?" She sighed, and that was when he noticed her waitressing uniform. "You work for Mac?"

"Yeah, I don't have much of a choice. The scholarship I won got hit by some kind of fraud thing, or the company behind it. My scholarship got taken away, and there's no way for me to continue. My folks can't afford it, so I'm back at home. I'm enrolled at the local college. It's not the same, but it's better than nothing."

"Shit, I'm so fucking sorry."

"Don't be. It's not like you could do anything about it."

"But it's what you always wanted to do."

She shrugged and smiled at the same time. "I can't stop what's happening, Matthew." She pointed at the ground. "What's with you smoking? Even when you were a cool kid you never smoked."

"I've decided to take it up as a hobby."

She chuckled. "Those things can kill you, you know, more than a gun."

"I don't know, I think I'd take the gun at this

point." Damn, she looked so incredibly beautiful. She had dyed her hair since the last time he saw her, and it was a deep red color.

"Anyway, I better go. I don't want to be late."

"How about I drive you? I'm not doing anything but sitting around on my ass."

"You should be studying."

"And now I'm going to drive you to work." He rushed around to the passenger side. "Climb in, princess."

She sighed. "Fine. Fine."

"What was the name of your scholarship again?" he asked.

She told him the name, and this time he smiled.

Luna would be going to college. First, he needed to talk to his father.

Chapter Three

"Oh fuck," Brass said. He stared down and watched as Eliza took his dick to the back of her throat. The moment they entered his place, she hadn't been able to keep her hands off him, not that he could deny her. She was fucking perfect.

His dick was covered in saliva, and she ran her hand up and down the shaft, removing her lips from the tip.

"Do you like sucking my cock?" he asked.

"Yeah, I do."

She was completely naked, and there wasn't a mirror in sight so that he could see her. In the past three weeks, he had already had mirrors installed in his bedroom so that he could see her in every single fucking direction.

"You're good at it."

She giggled. "You're just saying that."

This was what he found most baffling. When they were fully clothed, and had been apart for a few hours, everything seemed awkward, and wrong. Put them in a room, naked, and everything came out in the open.

"I'm not." He winked.

"I like Mary. She's so sweet. My dad is a complete asshole. I want to work, Brass. I don't want you to think that I'm here because you're paying my way. I'm not … easy."

He reached down, stroking her cheek. "I know you're not easy."

"It's not that. I just … for so long I've wanted to be independent of my father. I felt for the first time in my life that I could be, and now, I don't know. It's like I'll never get away from him, and that terrifies me. I don't want to marry Darcy, Brass. He's an asshole, and he's mean as well. I don't like him, and I don't want to go back to that way of life. I know a lot of people see me as a pampered princess and everything, but I don't want to be that. I want to just be Eliza, and nothing else."

Brass reached out and pulled her into his lap. He ran his hand down her thigh, loving the feel of her curves pressed against him. "I know you're not a pampered princess." Every time he came home he noticed that his place had been thoroughly cleaned. There was so much more to Eliza than just her name, and yet from the sounds of it, her name was the only thing that everyone has ever wanted from her. "While you are here, I will protect you."

She kissed his lips. "What about when my dad finds out?"

"What do you mean?"

"He's not the kind to let things slide, or to leave it alone. He will come here, possibly with Darcy, and when he does, he will cause problems."

"You're worried he's going to ruin some of the businesses of Vale Valley?"

"Yeah. It's what scares me about Mary and Holly's blog. He could ruin that."

Brass licked his lips and leaned back. "I'll take care of it."

"That simple?"

"I'm not going to lie, it's not going to be that simple, but leave it to me. I'll deal with your father, and with that asshole who thinks he can control you. I'm a Trojan, babe. I'm resourceful."

She chuckled, moving to straddle his lap. "I can't believe I'm doing this." She wrapped her arms around his neck, and started to grind down on his dick.

Eliza was so wet that he felt her cream on his shaft. He wasn't wearing a condom, and he knew they were both clean. He wanted to take her without a condom, and thought about Landon's little insight. If he did get her pregnant, he'd be able to keep her in Vale Valley forever.

Don't fucking do it, man.

Don't turn into Crazy's whore.

His fellow club brother Crazy had been caught by a club whore who had used her pregnancy to manipulate the brother. After she gave birth to Strawberry, she'd made Crazy's life hell until he met Leanna. Then everything changed.

What he was thinking right now was no different from her.

Grabbing Eliza's ass, he groaned, wanting nothing more than to slide into her wet cunt.

"I want you, Brass," she said, sinking her fingers into his hair.

The sound of the doorbell was a welcome relief even if it was a hated sound.

She gave a little squeak.

"Your future is here," he said, getting to his feet. He handed her a shirt and his boxers to cover herself, while he slid his jeans up his body. Only when he was sure she was covered, did he go to answer the door. Raoul, Landon, and Diaz were on the other side.

"You ask, and I deliver. It'll cost you, buddy," Raoul said.

"This shit is legal, right?"

"Of course," Diaz said. "All of it is fucking legal. I wouldn't do that to my Trojan boys. I value your business far too much."

"What is all this?" Eliza asked, coming up behind him. Her hair was all over the place, and she looked thoroughly fucked.

"This is so you can take up writing again."

"But my dad?"

"I'll take care of it. You can do whatever you want."

"Who is this young lady?" Diaz asked, staring at her. Of course he knew who she was. When she first came into town, they had run her name through the system via Diaz.

"Eliza, it's nice to meet you."

"The name's Diaz, lady, and whatever you need, you just give me a call." He handed her a card, and Brass took it away.

"She won't be needing any special product or shit. She's mine."

"She is?" Diaz asked.

Raoul slapped Diaz around the back of the head. "We're friends, but that doesn't mean you can sell on our turf."

"I know. I know."

Brass wrapped his arms around her shoulder, pulling her in close. "He's a friend of the club. You want to make some drinks? I'll get them to set this shit up for us."

"You're too good for me," she said.

He watched her go, knowing in his heart of hearts that she was too damn good for him.

Following Raoul, Landon, and Diaz into his office, he'd already cleared a desk so they could set it up for her.

"She's nice," Diaz said.

"You've spoken to her once," Brass said.

"Yeah, and the bitches I know would have taken that card, and asked for a bag of coke. Believe me, a good woman is hard to find, and in my line of work, they're all fucking druggies."

"You sell the drugs," Brass said.

"Yeah, so? You sell guns, but you don't want an old lady shooting up your shit, do you? I know the shit that goes into the product I sell. I've seen what it does, and I don't want any of it near my family. Call me a fucking old school kind of guy. I want a lady."

Brass was amazed. He would never have guessed it from Diaz. The guy was heavy in drugs, and his crew was known to be the worst around. Raoul was a close friend, and so through the two of them, the Trojans had formed an ally. It kept them close with information, and the shit off the streets.

While they were setting up the computers, Eliza came through with their drinks. He loved seeing her dressed in his clothes.

Time passed, and it seemed forever before the boys left his home.

Eliza was sitting behind her desk when he came back, and when he moved behind her, he saw she was already writing away. A document was open with the heading, "Chapter One".

"Wow, that was fast."

"Sorry. I just wanted to see if I could still do it. Ideas are always going around my head. Wow, this is real?"

"It is." He moved some of her hair off her neck, and began to kiss her pulse. She released a little moan and leaned back.

"That feels so good."

"I want to read what you write."

"Yes."

She stood suddenly, and moved into his arms. Sinking his fingers into her hair, he held her close as he pressed her up against the wall. "I want you on my bed, legs spread, and playing with your sweet pussy," he said.

Brass released her and watched as she made her

way out of his room. The shirt he'd given her dropped to the floor. He waited for a minute before following her. Picking up his shirt, and then the boxer briefs, he entered his bedroom. She was lying in the center, legs spread, and her fingers sliding between her slit, teasing her clit. His cock thickened, and it was a challenge to stay at the door, watching.

"Are you mine?" he asked.

"Yes."

"Then fuck two fingers inside that wet cunt." The curtains were open with the sunlight pouring through the window giving him the perfect view of her cunt. Her pussy was covered in a small smattering of curls.

Watching her fingers fuck inside her to the knuckle, made him wish it was his cock. She was always so tight, so hot, and so fucking perfect. He had fucked so many women over the years, and none of them had made them crave their bodies the way she did.

"Show me how wet you are."

She lifted her fingers for him to see.

"Finger your clit," he said, removing his jeans, and fisting his cock. The tip wept pre-cum, and he smeared it into the whole head, watching as she stroked her clit. Moving toward the edge of the bed, he knelt down, and flicked his tongue across her fingers, bumping her clit as he did.

"Don't stop." Releasing his cock, he spread the lips of her pussy wide, and watched as she filled her pussy. Taking her fingers, he sucked each digit into his mouth, moaning at her taste.

He slid two of his fingers inside her, and then worked a third finger. Her pussy stretched around his fingers, and he began to pump them inside her. He was so damn hard, and he wanted to fuck her until neither of them could think straight.

Eliza knelt up, wrapping one arm around his neck, and with the other she slid down his body, wrapping her fingers around his length.

"I love how hard you get."

Glancing down, he continued to finger-fuck her pussy, at the same time she worked his cock. She palmed the tip, and used the pre-cum to coat the whole of his shaft. It felt fucking good to have her hands on him.

She got as dirty as he did, and talked just as much.

"You like that?" she asked.

"You know I do."

She let his dick go, and moved his hand out of the way. He watched as she slid her fingers inside her, and then moved them to cover his cock, coating him with her own cum. It was erotic as fuck.

"When I'm with you, I feel I can do anything and there won't be any judgment," she said, licking her lips.

There would never be any kind of judgment from him. Brass wanted her to stay, and he was part of an MC that defied convention. They didn't stick to the set of rules they were told to. They had their own rules, and that was exactly what Brass lived by. Their code, not what he'd been told to live.

Sinking his fingers into her hair, he held her close, and smashed his lips against hers. He wanted to taste her, to make her forget every single man she had been with so she was only consumed with thoughts about him. Fuck, he wanted her so badly that it was all he could think about.

Never had a woman gotten under his skin this badly before.

Suddenly, he grabbed her hand and held it up to his lips, and he started to lick her fingers, tasting her. "You taste so fucking good."

In one swift move he had her on the bed with her

legs spread. Grabbing his cock, he circled the entrance of her cunt, and then slammed every single inch of himself to the hilt inside her, listening to her scream. Taking hold of her hands, he locked them either side of her head, holding her close. Staring into her eyes, Brass started to fuck her. He worked her body until she had no choice but to give him everything. He pulled out of her, and sank down the bed until his face was between her thighs. Licking her clit, he tasted her creamy pussy, sucking the hard nub of her clit into his mouth. He flicked his tongue over her and plunged his fingers deep inside, feeling her pussy tighten around him.

She was so close that with a few strokes of his tongue, she came on his fingers. Brass didn't waste any time. Moving up the bed, he found her pussy once again, and slid deep inside her, going to the hilt. Her pussy was still pulsing around his dick, and he fucking loved it. He loved the feel of her surrounding him. Taking her lips, he slid his tongue into her mouth, claiming her.

The need to take her as his own was so fucking strong inside him.

"Brass," she said, moaning his name.

That was what he wanted to hear. His name cried out from her lips, sheer fucking perfection.

He went from fucking her to making love, taking his sweet time with her body. She was the most beautiful woman he had ever seen. From the moment she entered the mechanic shop to now. She took his breath away, and made him ache for more.

There was no way he was going to let her go. She belonged to him, and as he followed her into ecstasy, Brass knew he was well and truly fucked.

****

"I think it's sweet that he got you a computer and stuff. Are you going to do it? You know, write?" Mary asked.

"Yeah, I want to. It's something I've always wanted to do, and I've always found a reason not to do it, so yeah, I think so. I don't want Brass to think that he's bought my stuff for nothing." Eliza stood in the kitchen of the Trojans MC clubhouse, and it was kind of surreal. She had seen completely naked women, semi-clad women, and then she'd seen what Mary had told her were the old ladies, who were treated like royalty. It was all a little strange. Like a separate community from what she was used to.

Her family would spit and curse one moment, and then a few seconds later hug the same person they'd been hating on. She had found it next to impossible to behave like that. Her father got so angry with her because she didn't play by the rules. The more she thought about it, the more she imagined Darcy was a punishment for not being a very good daughter.

"My dogs behave better than you."

"Your father has that much reach?"

"When he's got wealth behind him, he can do anything, even if he's not supposed to be able to. It sucks. I've spent my whole life knowing that he's always going to be one step ahead."

"Brass can take care of it, and he can take care of you."

She nodded. Brass rocked her entire world. There were moments, like now, when she felt uncomfortable with how easy it was for Mary to tell her that.

"Hey, guys, sorry I'm late. It has just been really busy," Holly said, entering the room.

"It's fine. This is Eliza."

"I know. We met before at Knuckles and Beth's wedding. It's great to see you again. I take it things with Brass are going amazingly well?"

"I think so." This was the first time she had been around two women who were asking her these kinds of questions. This was a whole new world for her.

"In that case he's doing a good job. I have to say I'm a little intrigued about you, Eliza. I don't know much other than the fact your father is a total bastard."

Her hands started to get sweaty. "There's not much to tell to be honest," she said. "I'm just a girl. You know?"

"There's more to you than just being a girl, sweetie."

She blew out a breath, and decided to not give a fuck. "Here goes. I'm the daughter of a rich businessman, and he is not known for being a very nice man. In fact, he wants me to marry a man who loves someone else, and every time I tried to set my own path, I was stopped. I'm scared that my father is going to do something to hurt you guys, and I'm not going to lie, I'm kind of scared."

Silence fell.

"Wow, you're a fucking morbid one," Zoe said.

"I thought that was me," a girl said, coming up behind Zoe.

"Nah, it's not possible. Hi, I'm Eliza," she said, extending her hand.

"Winter. Actually, the real name is Maya, but I'm Winter while I'm here."

Zoe covered her eyes and groaned. "Seriously, can't you just pretend that you want protection or something?"

"Sorry. I guess I just don't really care. Is that a bad thing?"

"Yes!" All of the women shouted the word at the young girl.

Winter, or Maya? Eliza didn't have a clue what she was going to think of her as. "It's nice to meet you."

"Yeah, yeah, nice to meet you, too." Maya looked close to tears, and Zoe wrapped an arm around her.

"Look, we care okay. It may not be something you're used to, but to us, we care, and it means a hell of a lot to us, okay?"

"Yeah, I get it. I do."

Holly sighed, wiping her hands on a towel. "You're going to cry?"

"No. I'm not going to cry. I haven't cried since I watched my father murder my mother, and I was eight years old. Believe me, tears do not come easily to me."

In fact, Eliza watched as the pain on her face seemed to fade away as if it wasn't there at all.

She had never seen anyone cut off their emotions like that, and become almost cold.

Maya sat down at the table, and Eliza watched as Mary nudged Holly's arm.

"Go talk to her." Mary whispered. Eliza stood close, which was why she could hear.

"What do I say?" Holly asked.

"She's your sister."

"Half-sister."

"You are not the bitch you're acting like here, Holly."

"You know I can hear you," Maya said, looking up. "You don't have to pretend to like me. I know my presence has caused a real shit-storm for you."

This time Eliza turned to Holly, and watched as she ran fingers through her hair. Mary simply gave her a pointed look.

"It's nothing, okay? I'm sorry. I just, I don't know what to do or to think, and right now, everything is crazy. It's all fucking crazy. For the longest time Russ has been my dad, and I didn't think that I could have another life."

"Abelli is no father. Russ, he sounds like a pretty

45

decent guy," Maya said.

"Then you don't really know him either. He can be an asshole. I find it harder to talk to him now than ever before. He lied to me, and I know he's hurt my mom as well. Not a physical hurt either. He cheated on her, and it lost her baby. I guess there are elements of the past we will never know."

Maya nodded and licked her lips. "I know about you. Abelli was always talking about you, and your mother. There were times he'd compare us."

"He had nothing to compare to, Maya. Don't let it get to you. He's an asshole, and I have met him."

Eliza saw Maya tense up. "I guess that was an interesting conversation."

"It was. Pretty intense."

Mary took Eliza's hand, and they headed into another room filled completely with food.

"Wow, this place is like your own supermarket."

"Yeah, the guys don't like cooking, so we told them that we would feed the entire house, providing they got the food for us. I imagine the food bill is out of this world. We're doing a big cook off today. Want to help?"

"I'd love to."

She watched as Mary picked up a wicker basket, placed it on her arm, and started picking random items off the shelf. Eliza did the same, seeing the variety of different beans, and pastas. There was rice and even quinoa. "They eat this?" she asked, holding up the bag.

Mary laughed. "Nah, they don't, but we still cook it in the hope that they will change their minds. Men are so stubborn. They do not eat quinoa."

"That was kind of intense back there," Eliza said.

"I can't really talk to you about the whole details of it. You're not an old lady, or one of the women they screw."

"Oh."

"No, I don't mean with Brass. Ugh, they call them club whores, sweet-butts, the girls they screw with no meaning to it. They have one purpose in life, to make the boys happy. I don't mind most of them, and I know Pike is faithful. The thing with Maya and Holly and the club, is it has some really personal problems attached to it. I'm just an old lady, and you haven't been brought in by Brass."

"No, no, no, of course. I didn't mean to pry. You and Holly are close, and you said they were sisters."

"They're half-sisters. Same dad but different moms. Anyway, I really can't discuss what is going on."

"That's fine."

"It's all on Brass and what he decides."

She picked a variety of cans and packets of food, heading into the kitchen.

"Can I try to cook something?" Eliza asked. Right now she wanted to do something with her hands, and distract her from how upset she was.

"Sure," Holly and Mary said.

She took her ingredients and made her way to the fridge, picking up random items. Eliza didn't have a clue what she was going to make or even if it was going to be edible. She found several cut up chickens, briskets, and other meats. So many fresh vegetables and herbs. It was crazy, but then, food bloggers for old ladies must be a bonus for these men. She grabbed one of the cut up chickens, and several vegetables, and went back to her work station. She didn't like how much Mary's words had hurt.

Chapter Four

Duke stared across the clubroom, and with the kitchen door partially opened, he watched his woman work her magic. The scents coming from the kitchen made his mouth water. No matter how much he tried to distract himself, this wasn't going to help in his decision about Abelli.

"You okay?" Pike asked, coming to stand beside him.

"Yeah, I'm fine. I'm watching our women." He smiled. "I remember sitting outside those damn doors, watching the two of them, wanting her for my own, and not knowing if I was ever going to keep her." He had come a long way from being jealous of Raoul. The love he had for Holly was fucking pure. She was the best thing that had ever happened to him.

"I know. I nearly lost Mary, and now I've got a kid. We've, erm, we've got another on the way, Duke. She doesn't want to tell anyone. Thinks it's bad luck."

"Congratulations." He shook his hand. "I don't know what to do."

"Yeah, you do. You just don't want to upset Holly. It's either Sheila or Russ, or we declare war with the entire Abelli family."

Duke looked at the floor. "I'm in contact with the head of the Abelli family."

"Wow," Pike said.

"Yeah. It seems Holly's father was out of favor, which is why no backlash has come from Russ's attack twenty years ago. As far as Daddy Abelli sees it, his son had it coming. Anton has a reputation for doing what he wants, and it's not to better the Abelli name. Francis doesn't like that. Every decision has to be made for the wealth and respect of Abelli. Twenty years ago, Anton was causing a lot of problems, severing ties left, right, and center. What Russ did, Francis considered it a job well done. It makes me wonder what kind of shit Anton was doing for a father to not care. If anyone did that kind of shit to Matthew, I wouldn't stop until their head was mounted on my wall."

"What are you hoping to do?" Pike asked.

"Deal with Francis Abelli. He's Holly's grandfather. I don't want to alarm her about this. I'm trying to do it under Anton's radar." Anton Abelli was Holly's father, and the one that had given him the ultimatum. "Make a deal with him, save Russ and Sheila's life, and while I'm at it, make a few deals that benefit the Trojans, and we all get to live another day to enjoy life and to fuck."

"You think you can do that?"

"Trojans are not to be messed with, and we're certainly not someone's messenger. I want to deal with this without much death. Anton doesn't give a shit about the Abelli name. He's after vengeance, and I think he's trying to make a statement to his father. I don't know. Either way, no one is going to die as far as I'm concerned."

"Is that why you've got Matthew home?" Pike asked.

"I've got no choice. I don't know how far his reach is. Once I do, I'll deal with it." This situation had to be handled properly, without much death, and if he could do that, he would.

"Hey, Dad, can I talk to you?" Matthew asked.

"Sure, follow me." Duke went into his office, and closed the door. "What's up?"

"Luna lost her scholarship."

"Oh, crap, I'm so sorry, son." He wasn't going to pretend that he didn't have a clue who Luna was. That girl nearly made him a granddaddy.

"Can we give it to her?"

"Excuse me?"

"I want to give Luna the money to go to college. Can't you get Diaz, or that lawyer Briars to do it?"

"And what exactly do you want me to do?"

"Pay for it. I know all she wants to do is go to college, and I want this for her, Dad. Please."

He stared at his son. Matthew had never been passionate about anything other than being a pain in the ass. There was something in his son's eyes, something he recognized. "You love her."

"Yeah, I do." Matthew didn't hesitate. "I want her to have everything her heart desires. Is that a bad thing?"

"No, of course not."

"I'll do anything. Scrub floors, clean out toilets, damn, I'll even mop up after the fucking orgies. I just want Luna to have what she needs."

"I'll look into it."

"You will?"

"Yeah, I will, but you keep that thing in your pants covered. I'm too damn young to be a granddad."

"You don't have to worry about that. Luna wouldn't let me touch her anyway."

"Then why are you helping?" Duke asked.

"Because I want to see her happy. I don't care what I do or don't get so long as she's happy."

His son was finally growing up, and for that, he was getting prouder by the day.

****

"Are you going to keep ignoring me?" Russ asked.

Holly paused, holding a plateful of herbs in her hands. The cook-off was going great, and for a few seconds, she didn't have to think about the decision that her own father wanted her to make.

"If you must know, I don't have a clue what to say to you," she said, turning to face him.

This was the man she had called father all of her life. The memories of Anton Abelli were so damn faint that it could easily be mistaken as a child's fantasy. "I'm still the same guy here, Holly."

"Are you? Really?" She sighed, and looked around the clubhouse yard. This had been her home, and yet it had all been a lie. "Everything is a lie in my life…" She couldn't bring herself to call him Dad. She blew out a breath. "I don't know what you want from me."

"I love your mother. I adored Sheila, and seeing how miserable she was, I couldn't allow that to happen anymore."

"So you scarred him, and took us."

"I did everything I could to make you guys safe. I took the Trojans and made sure they were to be feared and respected."

"Even as you did all of that, you didn't think about what the future would hold. Every year you grew older, and it was only a matter of time before someone else took over from you. You didn't think, Russ."

"Don't call me that," he said.

"What should I call you? Huh? Dad, you're not him. You're not my father, and you're not Russ. I don't know you, and I don't know Mom. The only people who have been completely honest with me are the men in this fucking club, and Duke. Damn, even Matthew is more honest with me, and he hides his damn porn from me. So please tell me what it is I can do for you. Honestly, because right now, Duke has been given a decision, and I don't know what to do."

"You'd even consider it?"

"You, Mom, or the club. You do the math, Russ."

She stared at the man, and all she felt was betrayed by him.

"I did what I thought was right."

"What *you* thought was right?"

"Yeah, I did. I did it for you and for Sheila, okay? I love her, goddamn it."

Holly started laughing. "You love her?"

"Yeah."

"Then tell me, Russ, why did you cheat on her, huh? Why did you make her life such a misery that I had to listen to her crying, knowing that you were with other women?" She watched him go pale. "Yeah, you see that's what I thought. Don't come here telling me what I should or shouldn't do. I'm avoiding you right now because it's easier that way, believe me. It's so much easier."

****

Brass sat at the club wondering what Eliza was doing. Mary had dropped her off earlier, and he had to stay for a club meeting.

"Hey, sugar, you okay?" Emma asked.

She was a club whore, and seemed to be one of the good ones. Not because of her ability to fuck, just because she seemed to care.

"I'm fine."

"I saw your girl today. She was in the kitchen. She's a pretty one."

"What do you want?" he asked, turning toward her.

"Nothing. I just wanted to say that if you need any help with her, I'll be glad to do it."

She touched his thigh, and Brass caught her wrist, pulling it off his leg. "No, Emma. I'm taken."

"You've not branded her. You branded me, remember?"

Emma was one of the women he'd screwed to

become a club whore. He sighed. "You going to cause me problems here, Emma?"

"How do you mean?"

"You know your place. You know what is required of you, and what is not. I need to know if you're about to cause me some trouble with Eliza."

"It's serious with her?"

"Yeah, it is. She's mine, and I may not have claimed her yet, but I will." It was just a matter of time before he made her his. "Do not overstep that mark again."

He got up, and made his way toward the bar. There was another Prospect on the bar, and he didn't have a clue what his name was. It seemed the boys trying to join them were because of some television show that showed their life. They just couldn't hack the time. He didn't care. He'd earned his patch fair and square.

"You okay?" Daisy asked, taking a seat beside him.

"I'm good. How are you?"

"Knuckles and Beth are heading out for their honeymoon next week. I don't have to see them smooching, so all is good in my world. Maria is of course, beautiful as always. Tanya is just wonderful." Tanya was his little girl.

"You've got it all."

"Yeah, I do. I never thought it was possible to be this happy to be honest." Daisy sipped at his coffee, which was also new. Ever since Daisy had married Maria, the hard partying lifestyle had stopped. A club meeting had never stopped him from an orgy or two.

"I want Eliza to be my woman," Brass said.

"Are you sure? It has only been a couple of weeks."

"I've never been more sure of anything else in my

life, Daisy. It's what I want, but I know I've got to wait, take my time."

"I heard through gossip that her father is a piece of work."

"He is. I'm stopping by to see Clinton tomorrow. Get some information on him."

Daisy shook his head. "I'd go to Raoul, and get him to go to Diaz. Clinton has to go through relevant channels that could alert her father. If he's a real piece of work, you don't want that happening. Diaz can do things discreetly."

Brass hadn't thought of it like that. "I'll do it."

"Pleased I could help."

Brass sipped at his own coffee, and watched the kid behind the bar. He was looking around the clubhouse in complete awe of everything.

"Kid, come here," Brass said.

"You're talking to a Prospect?"

"May as well. They're dropping like fucking flies around here."

The kid walked toward him, smiling. "Can I help you?"

"Yeah, why are you here?"

The smile didn't disappear. "I've been wanting to be a Trojan for a long time. I went to the high school with Matthew. I was a nerd, and I didn't think it was possible for someone like me to come here. I know computers, not much else. The past year I've been building hard, practicing. This is what I want. What I need."

Brass tilted his head to the side and stared at the kid. He had passion that was damn sure, and he hadn't been determined to make him remember his name.

"So this isn't just some game to you."

"Nah, it's not. From when I was a little boy I wanted to be a Trojan, man. You guys, you do real shit, and you band together. I want that. I really do."

Brass noticed that he moved to cover his arms. They were kind of thin, but Brass saw the silvery marks. Cigarette burns.

"Your dad did that?" he asked.

"Dad, Mom, his friends. I was just a toy to amuse themselves with. I got out of the foster system when I was eighteen. I stayed out near the school."

Brass knew of the foster care home near the school. They donated money to it every single year to help kids without parents.

"I don't complain. I'll do anything. I've heard the rumors that everyone thinks Prospects are here for the pussy, and drink and stuff. That's not me. I don't care for the sex, or anything. I just … I want a family. Guys who I know will have my back no matter what."

Brass nodded, and when he glanced over at Daisy, he saw he was just as impressed. "Keep everything up, do as you're told, and there might be hope for you yet."

Duke clapped his hands, gaining their attention. "Church now."

Brass followed his brothers as they all entered the main clubroom where their table stood. This had been the table that Russ once sat at. Glancing around the room, Brass noticed Russ wasn't there, which was a first. He was usually all over this shit. Taking his seat, he glanced over at Duke.

"First, no matter what you're going on your honeymoon, brother," Duke said, looking at Knuckles.

"Not if you need me."

"I don't need you. What I need is for men to do as I've asked. I want you to take your woman, and give her what she deserves. She's been patient, and I'm a man of my word. Go, and have some fun. That's the last I hear on it, understand."

"Yes."

"Good." Duke ran a hand down his face. "As I'm sure many of you noticed, Russ isn't here."

"Just a little bit," Raoul said.

"You're all aware of the threat that Abelli has made, and what Russ did to him. You're also aware of Holly's true parentage, and I want to thank you all for not treating her any differently."

"Holly's part of this club, Duke. It doesn't matter who her father is. She's as much a Trojan as the rest of us," Pie said.

They all agreed. Most of them had watched Holly grow up, and she was such a sweet woman.

Strong, independent, and she had taken Duke's son Matthew, and helped raise him as her own. Considering there was only a handful of years between the two, that was a pretty gutsy thing to do.

"Thank you. That means everything to me. Holly and I, we went to see Abelli, and he has an ultimatum."

"Wait, when did you go to see Abelli?" Pike asked.

"A couple of nights ago."

"And you didn't think to take one of us with you. That man is a fucking pyscho."

"I wasn't about to start a possible war. I wanted to know what Abelli's cards were, and we laid our shit out on the table." Duke ran fingers through his hair.

"You know the shit he did to Winter, and now you're telling me you sat down and talked with him, and he's not fucking dead?" Landon asked.

"He knows she's here, Landon. We may as well call her Maya."

"You didn't answer my question."

"You want me to put this entire club, and the life of my woman at risk, then I will gladly go back and take that piece of shit out," Duke said, standing up and slamming his hand on the table. "This is not just about one man. If I don't handle this shit properly, then everyone dies. Zoe, Mary, Leanna, Maria, and Beth, even Eliza," he said, looking at Brass. "My son, our kids, everyone. I don't know the reach and the pull of the Abelli fortune."

"Why haven't they done that already?" Chip asked. The brother rested his head on his hands, looking a little bored. His arms were covered in ink, and not that tribal shit either. Each picture was a tale of death and destruction on his skin.

"Our reputation. I truly believe that. We have the best that there is. Our enemies have all turned up dead. Besides, Abelli wants something more than our heads." Duke looked around the table. "He wants either Russ or Sheila, along with Maya's silence. If he gets that, he goes away."

They all fell silent. Giving up a brother went against everything that they were.

"You can't do that, Duke," Pike said.

"I know I can't do that. I've been in contact with Francis Abelli. He's reasonable and Holly's grandfather." Duke started laughing. "He will control his son providing he gets the chance to meet his granddaughter and great-grandkids. Where his son has gone fucking loopy, he's a family man."

"Is that all?" Crazy asked. "I'm sorry, but a big time guy like Abelli won't just want to meet his grandkids. What else does he want?"

Duke paused. "He wants to work with the Trojans. He likes the thought of having us as backup. Our reputation precedes us."

"He wants us to work for him now?" Landon asked.

"Look, I know you're pissed, Landon. I fucking get it, okay? I do. I'm not talking about working with Anton. I'm talking about working with Francis, and I believe him when he says that he had nothing to do with arranging Maya's attack. He'll deal with Anton. We get called up to do some of his work. We get paid, and paid well. It's a win-win as far as I'm concerned."

Brass looked toward Landon, and saw the brother shaking his head. "Abelli needs to pay for what they did to her."

"I know," Duke said. "Our options are limited with this. I won't act on this now, but I will have to. You can guarantee it. Francis has no interest in harming Maya. I'm doing this for her, for Russ and Shelia, for my woman. I'm doing this for the club. I need you guys to understand this. Anton acts without his father's permission. There's only so much hold a person has. Please, think about this."

****

Eliza clapped her hands and giggled as the flour created a puff of smoke and stuff. For the first time in her life she was free, and she felt it more now than ever before. After making the dish at the clubhouse, she had come home, and decided to make her and Brass a chicken pot pie. The crust was tricky to do, but she loved it. She had watched the cook at her family home make it many times, and it was a relief to make it herself.

Even though Mary's words had hurt her, Eliza decided not to take it too personally. Brass hadn't declared her as his old lady, and she wasn't about to cry over something she didn't have a clue on.

Spooning the chicken mixture into the pots, she topped them with her pie crust, and after brushing them with an egg wash, she placed them in the preheated oven. Now it was the cleanup.

ASY

Once the kitchen was clean, she made her way back toward her computer, and stared at the screen, which showed her latest story. She had already written a quick romance story. It had been a couple of years since she last wrote anything, so she was building back up, trying to gain her confidence in the written world once again. Clicking her fingers out like she had seen many times in the movies, she put her fingers on the keys, and allowed the magic to take over.

She was writing about a lonely mechanic and a woman who had broken down in his town. Yeah, it was totally her and Brass's story. The beginning of it at least, and it was nice to kind of document it.

For many years she had given up on love, and the prospect of any kind of romance. Nothing was allowed in her life unless her father had taken care of it first.

When the door opened and Brass called out to her, she saved the story, and made her way toward him, and found him hanging up his jacket. He looked a little stressed, and she didn't know why. She went straight into his arms, hugging him.

"Shit is about to hit the fan, baby."

"I'm here." She wanted to be here. Brass had come into her life, and blown her world, and now she didn't want to go.

His hands moved behind her back, holding her close. "I'm not going to lie to you, this could get ugly."

She leaned back so that she could see him. "Do you want me to leave?" The moment she said those words, he held her a little tighter, his hand fisting in her shirt.

"No, I don't want you to leave."

"Then I'm not going anywhere. I'm not the kind of person to cut and run." She sank her fingers into his hair. "You've got me until you get rid of me."

9

His hand moved toward her ass and gripped it tightly. She released a little moan, loving his hands all over her. "I'm not getting rid of you, ever, baby. You're all mine, and it's going to stay that way."

Before she could respond, his lips slammed against hers, and then there was absolutely no way of her fighting. She wanted him as much as he wanted her.

Chapter Five

Three days later

Brass had seen Knuckles and Beth off last night for their honeymoon, and Duke had declared no more parties until further notice. Duke was going out of town for a few days with Holly and the kids. He wasn't an idiot. All of the club knew what he was going to do, and they were behind him.

There was no way that they would ever accept Anton Abelli in their lives, or to take one of their own. It wasn't going to happen. Maya Abelli was also going to be under their protection. When Duke got back they would have to talk to Clinton and Maya about what she was willing to testify to. Landon wasn't happy, and he refused to let her go. She was his responsibility, and no one was going to hurt her while he was watching her.

A feminine sigh made him turn to his own little problem. Well, not problem, Eliza was a complete pleasure. Something was holding her back, and he knew without a doubt that it had to do with her father, so he was going to try to get to the bottom of it. He'd gotten Raoul onto Diaz to find out as much as possible about them. The more he knew about them the happier he would be.

Tucking a strand of her hair out of the way, Brass ran his finger across her full lips. Last night they had been wrapped around his cock driving him toward an earth shattering orgasm. Sex had been off the cards last night as she was on her monthly cycle. He was more than happy to wait and snuggle. She had wanted to give him something, and he wasn't about to complain.

"You're watching me sleep again," she said, opening her eyes, and smiling at him.

"I can't resist."

She chuckled and stretched. The blanket pulled down revealing her large tits. This time he groaned, and cupped one mound. "I love your tits," he said.

He loved it when she pressed her tits together, and he fucked between them. His cock awakened at the memory of fucking her tits.

Leaning down he captured her nipple and sucked in the hard bud.

Her chuckle turned into a gasp. Her fingers sinking into his hair and holding him close.

He pushed the blanket out of the way, and the sight of her panties had him pausing.

"I can take care of that for you," she said.

"No. I can wait, and speaking of waiting, I want to take you out away from here."

"Where are we going?" she asked.

"We are going to the beach. Do you think you can handle the back of a bike for a couple of hours?"

She gave a little squeal. "A beach?"

"Yeah. I think it's time we got out of Vale Valley for a few days."

He saw the excitement in her eyes slowly start to fade until it was gone completely.

"What is it?" he asked.

"I just, what if he can cause us some trouble? My dad?"

"It's not going to happen. We'll be back by tomorrow evening. I've already booked a reservation at a motel. It's nothing classy, but it'll just be me and you." He saw she was still panicking. "How about I tell the brothers and that way they'll be a phone call away if it scares you that much."

"Being alone with you doesn't scare me, Brass."

"You father, I know. Have you ever thought that he's not just a businessman?"

"What do you mean?"

"His pull on everyone around him. He took down an entire publishing company. Doesn't that strike you as a bit too much power for a random businessman?"

She sighed. "I would, but if I tell you that he's one of the few billionaires around, and he's old money as well. He's … strict."

Brass was going to look into him anyway. Something didn't feel right. It could be that he was just rich, which was how he was able to have so much sway with everyone. Diaz couldn't come through fast enough for him.

Pressing his lips against her, he cupped her waist, plunging his tongue into her mouth. She melted against him, and he loved her soft curves. He gave her a final kiss, and climbed out of the bed, pulling her up with him. "Come on. The sooner we get on the road, the better."

She giggled, following him into the bathroom.

After using the toilet, he washed his hands, brushed his teeth, and headed out to give her privacy. Pulling up a pair of boxers followed by jeans, he padded into the kitchen, picking up his cell phone.

There was a missed call from Raoul, and he dialed him back.

"What's up?"

"So I just got off the phone with Diaz. It turns out your guy is the shit. He's richer than most people combined."

"His business is all legit?"

"Every single cent. He's got businesses all over the globe, and then some. Seriously, this guy has it all everywhere. Also, he's a major control freak, and he's not so squeaky clean on the home front. Diaz found he had mistresses in each city. He has a clean family man image, yet he's got several bastards all around the country."

"Do you think Eliza knows?"

"Nope. Not a chance. Bishop has a reputation for control. He demands it, and right now he's focused on joining forces with the guy that Eliza's supposed to marry. Two names brought together as one."

Brass thought about that for a second. "Check him out, please. I want to know if he's got any bad shit around him."

"Will do. This will all cost money, and this is not club business, Brass."

"I already know this is personal shit, and I'm paying. You pay Diaz, and I'll pay you back." He hung up his cell phone just as Eliza walked into the kitchen. She was wearing a pair of jeans, and a really long baggy shirt. He had come to see that she rarely wore anything that hugged those curves of hers, and she wasn't all that confident in displaying them either, which was such a shame because her curves were fucking glorious. He loved holding onto them, and driving deep inside her pussy.

Down, boy. No action today.

He was going to prove to her that they could spend time together without sex. Brass wasn't just interested in banging her. He wanted it all, and if it made him sound like a pussy then so be it.

"Am I okay?" she asked, holding her arms out and giving him a chance to look.

Yeah, she was more than fine because they were going out in public, and it was just warming up a little. Spring would be with them soon, but it was still cold out. He wouldn't have to worry about men ogling her body because she never put it on display.

That's a good thing.

Brass wasn't handling all the jealousy that well,

not anymore.

"You look perfect. Let's get some breakfast, and head out."

"Okay."

They settled on some toast and coffee, and were on the road within twenty minutes. Brass loved being on his bike. It fucking rocked his world, and was way more freeing than a car. In a car, he wouldn't have Eliza's arms wrapped around him with her body flush against his chest. No, he'd have her beside him, and that just wouldn't do.

Making several stops along the way to freshen up helped, and he noticed that her legs got a bit stiff by the third stop.

"You okay, babe?" he asked.

"This is my first time riding a bike at all." She ran fingers through her hair trying to avoid having it shaped like the helmet he forced her to wear.

"You like it?"

"Hell yeah, it's so amazing. Even when you're doing the bends. I've never felt so alive." She released a little chuckle and headed into the toilets. He filled his bike up, and paid for it. By the time he got back, she already had the helmet back on and was waiting.

The next time he stopped, they were at the beach. Considering it was spring with a bite in the air it was still busy. Climbing off, he took the helmet from her, securing it to his bike. Once everything was set up, he grabbed her hand, and headed toward the beach.

"This is so perfect," she said, snuggling against him. It was just after eleven, and it was starting to warm up a bit. They walked along the edge of the ocean, and Brass wrapped his arm across her back, cupping her hip.

"Thank you for coming with me today."

"It's no hardship believe me. I love coming to the

beach, but I don't get the chance to be here all that often."

"You dad is a big time businessman, right?"

"Yeah. I'm surprised he hasn't used every opportunity to get you working for him," Brass said.

"He's old fashioned. He believes a woman's place is in the home and nowhere else. I don't think he employs that many women, and tries to avoid it if he can. Last time I was in his office, I saw three women total, and they were all dealing with coffee."

"Your dad sounds like a real shit." He had a lot more words to describe him, but as it was, he was going to keep them to himself.

"Can we not talk about him? He scares me enough as it is."

Brass tensed. "He ever hurt you?"

"Not in the physical way. Just with how much reach he has. It scares me of what he can do to you guys, and I like the Trojans MC. I know I'm nothing special. I'm not an old lady or a club whore, or even a patched in member, but I still care about what happens to you."

He glanced down at her, and she was staring straight ahead. There was something in her voice. He wasn't entirely sure what it was, but it did sound a little like pain. Did it hurt her?

Silence fell between them, and he didn't know what to fucking say. He wanted her as his old lady, but so far she hadn't shown any signs of commitment.

****

His silence sucked big time. Eliza couldn't even look at him as she felt tears fill her eyes, and that was no good. He didn't need to know how much his silence affected her. She wasn't good enough for her father, and now she wasn't good enough for Brass. She wasn't good enough for Darcy. She needed a dick to be good enough for him.

What did Brass want? She was afraid to ask because what if he didn't want anything, and he just wanted to have some fun?

"Eliza, have you even considered being my old lady?" He stopped, and she turned to face him.

"Yes, I have. I know we're moving fast, and that it seems almost too crazy to think about the future right now, but I know I love being around you, Brass. Even though you *did* tell me a little white lie." They had gone to her hotel as he had said to her in the beginning that he didn't have an apartment. Of course that was a total lie. He did have an apartment, and she now lived there. Before she'd moved in, he divided his time between the apartment and the clubhouse. Now he spent all of his time at the apartment, and he never invited her to the clubhouse.

She did feel like he was holding back part of his life, but there was nothing she could do about that.

"Being part of the club means that if your dad comes to town you can't leave, Eliza. An old lady, it comes with a great deal of responsibility."

Should his words be scaring her? No, she wanted to be part of the Trojans. She had seen them around town, including the way they were with their women. She was so damn envious of the women that were taken. They were loved and protected, taken care of. Everything she wanted in life they had, and she wanted to be part of it but also knew that it was next to impossible to have for herself.

"Forget it. It's fine. We're just having fun right?" she asked even though her heart was breaking. She wasn't going to force Brass to do something he really didn't want to do. This was the story of her life, and she wasn't about to overstay her welcome.

When she made to pull away, he held onto her

hand. "No, it's not just fun. You know that, and so do I. We both know what we want, and I'm not going to back down anymore. I want you, Eliza, and I want you as my old lady. All you've got to do is commit to me, totally to me, and forget about the life with your father. It's over with him, and that asshole Darcy. You'll belong to me. Everyone here will know that you belong to me. No holding back."

She stared into his eyes. There was no doubt in her life. "Yes. It's what I want."

He cupped her cheek and tilted her head back, running his thumb across her bottom lip. "There are a few things I need to tell you before you completely commit." Just like that her stomach started to growl. It was time for some food. "Let's get something to eat."

"That sounds so much better. Yes, please, food." She was a little nervous about what he was about to say, but nothing could be as bad as marrying a guy who doesn't even want to have sex with you.

They found a very old style diner, and Brass made sure they were in a secluded booth. When she picked up the menu, her mouth watered at the food on offer. She was so going to have a burger, and right now she needed one.

Once they had ordered their food, she focused all of her attention on Brass. "What's the big secret?" she asked.

"Most of the guys tend to keep their woman in the dark until the very end. I'm going to give you a chance to change your mind. So, the club has a rule when they deal with old ladies."

"What is it?"

He ran fingers through his hair, and she was starting to get even more nervous. Did they demand blood, a sacrifice? There was no way she was doing anything crazy.

"Don't judge. We have two ways of dealing with club women. When we take a club whore and she becomes the property of the club, a minimum of five guys screw her as the club watches. She's club property, and no one else can touch her."

She wrinkled her nose. "That's not an old lady, right?"

"Right. For an old lady, I would have to have sex with you while several of the club brothers watch."

Okay, she didn't hear right.

"What?"

"They become the property of the brother who claimed them, and all the brothers know she's not to be touched, but she is to be taken care of."

Eliza couldn't believe what she was hearing. She heard that MCs were all different, and all crazy, and this was so farfetched it was totally unbelievable. "You can't be serious. There is no way a woman would ever agree to that."

He sighed. "Every single old lady has done it, Eliza. It allows us to know that they are dedicated to their man, and to the club. Any woman who can do that, well, let's just say to us they have a lot of respect."

They were interrupted by the waitress bringing them their food.

"But I'm not really good," she said, pointing at her body.

Brass frowned at her. "I don't get it."

"I have a fat ass, Brass. No offence, but I'm not going to be laughed at or made a joke out of."

She wanted to burst into tears. Her hope of ever having a relationship with Brass was dying with each passing second. There was no way she could handle the thought of the men laughing at her.

"Babe, that would never happen." He reached out, grabbing her hand. "You are beautiful, Eliza. The guys, they wouldn't make you feel nervous, or anything. Have you seen Holly, Mary, Zoe, Leanna?"

She hadn't noticed.

"Every single brother would kick their ass if they hurt their woman, and that is the same with you. I would hurt anyone that hurt you."

"I'm going to lay my cards on the table here, Eliza. I'm all in. Are you?"

Holy shit!

Eliza stared at him. Even as their food was getting cold Brass didn't look away once. This was it, all or nothing. She didn't want to go anywhere but forward, and even though it terrified her, she knew her life was with Brass.

Life didn't have to be planned or easy. She would rather spend the rest of her life with Brass than with Darcy.

If she was truthful, she was starting to fall for Brass. He never held anything back, and he was always giving. He was considerate, and everything she wanted in a man.

Taking hold of his hands, she nodded. "I'm all in."

There was no way she was holding back anymore.

Chapter Six

"Your favorite color is brown, seriously?" Brass asked.

"Yeah. There's nothing wrong with it. I don't know, it's dark, and goes everywhere, don't you think?"

"Are we talking furniture here?" He grabbed a donut out of the warm bag and handed her one.

"No, well yes, well, maybe. I don't know. Brown furniture goes everywhere. Think about it, a lime green room, brown would work, but something yellow might not, and we're talking a really horrible yellow as well. Nothing good or nice."

He started to laugh and grabbed his own donut. "You're a screwball. Girls are supposed to like pinks and red and shit like that."

"Call me unconventional. What about you? What is your favorite color?" she asked.

His cock thickened as he watched her licking off the sugar on her fingers. They had been at the beach for the past three hours, and he didn't want it to end. Not one bit. The club already knew he wasn't heading back, as he'd told them before he left that he was staying out. He wanted some drama free time away with Eliza.

There had been no word from Duke, and as far as Brass was concerned, he was going to take the break while he could. He had a feeling shit with Abelli was going to go south very fucking quickly.

"You know that red underwear you wore the other day?"

"The one that is completely covered in lace?" she asked.

"That's the one. Yeah, that is my favorite color right now, and believe me, I'm not going to change it. In fact, we're going to buy you as many different reds as I can afford." And he could afford a lot.

She chuckled. "What's the point? You tore those off me, and I had to throw them in the trash. Everything you buy will just have to go there as well."

"It would still be money well spent."

He handed her another donut, and she sighed. "How am I going to diet around you?"

"You're not. It's simple, I love your ass with a jiggle to it, and I expect you to keep it that way." He reached behind her and gave her ass a squeeze. "God, I love it." He did, and one day he was going to fuck her ass as well. He was going to have her begging for more, and relish every single sound she made as he claimed that one final part of her.

"Don't you think we should be heading back? It's getting cold." She rubbed her hands together, trying to make them warm.

He covered them with his own, and blew on them. "Yeah, let's get to that hotel." He had booked the hotel in advance, but he hadn't told the club until a few hours ago that he was staying overnight. He didn't want to worry them.

Heading back to the bike, he tossed the last of the donuts away before handing Eliza the helmet. He found her so cute wearing it. Even though he was an expert rider, he wasn't going to risk it. She was going to be protected in all things.

"Do I have to wear this?"

"Yes."

"Why don't you have to?"

"Because I'm awesome."

"You're saying that I'm not?" she asked.

"No. I'm saying that you don't know how to ride, and until you do, you're wearing the helmet."

"Okay, fine, but it still sucks. Oh, I could ask

Landon to give me lessons."

He paused, and turned to glare at her. "Landon?"

"Yeah, I heard he was giving Zoe lessons, or was Raoul giving her lessons and Landon just watching?" She frowned and then shrugged. "I'd be good at riding a bike."

"The only bike you'll be riding is mine, and you're not taking lessons. You wear the helmet, and that is the end of that." He patted her head, and she shoved his hand out of the way. Climbing on the bike, he patted the seat behind him. "Get on, sweetie pie."

"I'm going to learn to ride."

He loved it when she had fire inside her. "We'll see."

Her thighs squeezed his legs, and he chuckled. There was no way her father could ever burn out that fire inside her. Eliza may not think it but she was filled with passion, fire, and he was going to relish drawing more of it out of her. He was never going to let her withdraw from him. Whatever her father or Darcy had to throw at him, he'd take it, and throw shit right back.

Pulling away from the beach, he parked outside of the hotel, and waited for her to climb off. Taking the helmet from her once again, he headed into the main reception holding her hand.

"What if they have no rooms?" she asked.

"I booked ahead, babe."

"Oh."

He released her hand long enough to pull out his wallet to pay for the room. Taking the key, he left the main reception and went toward their room. They were on the third floor right at the end. He liked the privacy.

Entering the hotel room, he closed the door behind her, and immediately pressed her against the door. Sinking his fingers into her hair, he held her captive against his body. Plunging his tongue inside her mouth, he ravished her lips, doing to her mouth what he wanted to do to her cunt.

Running his hands all over her, he groaned, knowing nothing was ever going to be enough, not to him.

"I love your hands on me," she said, pulling away from the kiss.

Suddenly, she caught his hands, and made him stop. He frowned, and watched as she sank to her knees before him. "What are you doing, babe?" he asked.

"What does it look like I'm doing?"

"You don't need to do that for me."

"I want to do it." She sat back on her feet. "Don't you want me to do it?" she asked.

"More than anything."

Eliza began to unbuckle his belt. "Then let me do this for you. It doesn't have to be a give and take. Sometimes it can be give, give, give, and other times it can be take, take, take."

She pulled his pants down until his cock sprang free. He groaned as her hand wrapped around his length running from the base up to the tip then back down. Closing his eyes, he tried to focus on not coming too soon.

He wasn't some horny teenager who didn't know how to deal with his shit. This was going to last. She licked the tip of his cock, tasting his pre-cum, and swallowing it down. She let out a little moan that only served to arouse him.

Forcing his eyes open, he watched as she worked the entire length of him with her hand, and licked the tip, swallowing down his pre-cum.

"Do you want me to stop?" she asked.

"No, not a fucking chance." Stroking her hair, he

twirled the strands through his fingers, groaning as she took the entire tip of him into her mouth. She didn't stop there, taking more of him to the back of her throat, and pulling back out.

She bobbed her head, and he held her head in place, knowing when he could, he was going to lick her pussy out, and have her screaming his name. He wasn't going to stop until she was begging, and then he was going to fuck her until she couldn't walk straight for days.

Just thinking about driving his cock deep into her cunt sent him over the edge.

"Oh, fuck, baby, I'm going to come," he said.

She didn't pull away, and he came, filling her mouth up with his seed. He watched her as she swallowed every single drop, and licked her lips, cleaning away any that had seeped out of the sides. It was so fucking sexy watching her do that.

He ran his thumb across her lips, and stared into her eyes. "I can't give you anything."

"You don't have to." She pressed a kiss to his hip. "There are going to be times that I want to give you something. Don't always think I'm after something because I'm not." She stood up, and kissed his cheek.

****

Later that night, Eliza was lying on the bed in only a pair of underwear while Brass read out one of her old stories. She had sent one of them in an email, and he was just now reading it.

"So, this guy, he's a complete asshole?" Brass asked.

"Yes, he is. What do you think?" she asked.

"I'm wondering how the fuck he can be deemed a hero. He's a bully. When did you write this?"

Her cheeks were staring to heat up. "A few years

ago, actually. I kept it secret. I never submitted that one. It was for my personal pleasure, you know. Getting out all that was locked inside."

Brass stared at his phone, and sighed. "Did you try to leave your father?"

"Yes. Lots of times. This was the first time I was ever successful." She pushed some hair out of her face. "Let's not talk about that."

"You're still worried though."

"Of course I'm worried. When you live with a man who always gets what he wants no matter what, it makes you feel a little afraid."

She watched as Brass licked his lips. "I had a friend look into your father."

"Oh, to see if there was anything you could hold against him?" she asked, and he nodded. "Well that's easy. No of course not. He's squeaky clean. I doubt there is an ounce of dirt on him or his image."

"You see, that's where you're wrong," he said.

"What do you mean?" She locked her fingers together, and stared right up at him.

"Your father doesn't lack female company, and it's not always your mother either. I've got a guy who was able to find his mistresses all over every state. Not to mention all of the kids he's helped create as well. You've got some half brothers and sisters walking around."

She tensed up, and her mother dropped open. "You're kidding."

"Nope. I was thinking about getting the guy to make a file on the women, the past women, and the kids that he has walking around. Would that help?"

Eliza frowned. Would it? Her father always talked about being a respectable human being, with high morals.

"Yeah, I think that could help. Anything that could risk his image, would be useful." She reached out, touching him arm. "You're being serious about this, aren't you? You're all in?"

"Yeah, I am, and not because you suck my dick either. I'm all in because the moment you walked into my life at the mechanic shop, I couldn't fucking think."

She laughed remembering his short answers and intense stare. It was the first time she had ever been looked at. Really looked at, and not just overlooked either. He'd made her feel visible when all of her life she had been invisible. She was to be not seen and not heard. Her father wanted her to shut up and do as she was told.

"I thought you were disgusted with me or something. I had no idea until you approached me that it had anything to do with this, between us." She pointed between them, and smiled.

He reached out tucking a strand of her hair behind her ear. "You blew me away." He glanced down at the bed before returning his gaze to her. "I'm not good with the whole romantic words and shit. To be honest I don't even know if they work or anything. Actions speak for me, but I'm really pleased your bag of shit car broke down."

Eliza couldn't wipe the smile off her face, or stop the butterflies in her stomach. "You didn't need to add the bag of shit car."

Brass shrugged. "It was, and I'm grateful for it. I want you to keep it so that it's a memory."

A memory for what? Their kids? Was he thinking that far ahead?

Instead of voicing her thoughts, she merely smiled, and in her heart, she hoped, she begged, that maybe, just maybe, they were on the same path.

****

"I'll do it," Maya said.

Landon paused, and stared down at the young girl.

She was sixteen years old, and had been through more hell than he could ever imagine. "What?"

"I told you. I'll do it. I'll agree to it providing I can stay here. If you don't want me here I can get my own place. That's all I want, to pave a life for myself far away from that world. I don't want any part of it. Guarantee me that, I'll keep my mouth shut."

He couldn't believe it, but then knowing what he did, and seeing the way she was, he could totally understand it. "I can protect you, Maya."

"I know. You all can protect me and I know what I promised to do, but if Granddad can keep him away, then that is what I want. He's the only one that can talk sense into him, and he wouldn't know what happened to me. In fact, he would get really, really mad at him." Maya pushed her hair off her face, and blew out a breath. "I know you're disappointed in me."

"I'm not disappointed." He moved to sit beside her on the sofa. Landon placed his arm across her shoulders, and pulled her in for a hug. There was nothing sexual in his feelings, or his actions toward Maya. He wasn't joking around when he said he saw her as a sister, and nothing more. All he wanted was to protect Maya, and allow her to have one hell of a good life. Not to be worried about the men who attacked her before. That shit was over with.

"You are."

"No. I don't like the thought of those men being left alive," Landon said. He didn't like it, and he had gone through her file, and every single bit of information that Clinton had without giving the game away that he was in fact hunting.

Everyone saw him as the fun-loving college boy. He was not a college boy any longer, nor was he pretending anymore. Maya was the sister he never had, and he wanted to protect her, which meant going hunting.

"Landon, I don't want anything to happen to you."

"Nothing is going to happen to me. Give me the names of the men who did this, and I will do everything I can to make sure you have a life away from the Abelli name. That's all I ask."

They stared at each other, and Landon refused to close his eyes. He was determined to win this. She sighed. "Fine. All of the close bodyguards to my father. That is who you're dealing with. They are deadly, trained to keep someone alive in the utmost pain so that they can torture them some more."

If she thought she was scaring him, she was wrong. He loved a good fight, a challenge.

He pressed a kiss to her head, and sat back.

"I heard some of the club say they're worried that you have feelings for me," Maya said.

Landon glanced over at her to see her biting her lip, the telltale sign that she was worried. "Yeah, I know."

"Do you have feelings for me?" she asked.

"Do you *want* me to have feelings for you?" he asked. He wasn't about to hurt her feelings.

"No, I don't. I care about you, Landon. You're sweet, and you're like a brother I never had."

He smiled. "Good, because that is exactly how I feel, only you're the sister part, not the brother part." He gave her a wink, and they sat together, staring at the blank screen of the television.

"Is it wrong I don't want him to pay, and I just want to be left alone?" she asked.

"It's not wrong. I get why you don't want to go after him. Believe me, I do." All she wanted was a life away from the Abelli clan. Was it really too much to ask?

Chapter Seven

Their trip was over, and now they were back in Vale Valley. Brass watched as Eliza walked around the house, putting a few of her feminine touches … finally. He had expected her to put some of her own mark on his place from the moment he got her out of the hotel room, but she hadn't. His space had remained permanently his. Did it make him a pussy that he wanted to have his woman mark his place? Should he ask his club brothers?

"What are you thinking about over there?" Eliza said, moving toward him, and hugging him close.

"You finally settling down with me, and then wondering if I'm a pussy."

She burst out laughing. "It's a little strange, but it makes you that perfect guy." She pressed her lips against his, and he sank his fingers into her hair. He felt the instant she melted against his body, and he fucking loved it.

"Why?"

"Because you want me to be part of your space. You're not going crazy because I'm putting my stuff in places that you hate." She stroked his cheek. "I like you, Brass."

It wasn't words of love, but he could live with that.

Brass paused. *Whoa!* When did he start thinking about fucking love? Shit! Staring into Eliza's eyes, he felt something deep in the pit of his stomach, and it wasn't revulsion. The thought of living without her filled him with deep sadness and regret.

"What is it?" she asked.

"Nothing."

"You look a little sick. You've gone pale. Do you think it was something you ate?"

He pulled away. "No, it's nothing. I just remembered I need to head out. I'm due at the shop. I'll see you here tonight though, right?"

"Yeah, I'm not going anywhere. I'm going to stay right here. Have a good day." When she went to press a kiss to his cheek, Brass couldn't help it and so he pulled away. He couldn't deal with this right now, and it was having a really strange effect on him.

"I've got to go." He'd hurt her when he pulled away. He knew that, and still, he walked right out of his apartment toward his bike, and was on the road within minutes, riding toward the mechanic shop.

The only thing he could do was clear his head. Love was a very strong, very deep emotion. He'd never been in love before, and now he was thinking about forever with a woman, and he had grown to care about her.

He wasn't a complete fucking idiot. The jealousy he felt toward fucking Darcy made things clear to him. Did he want forever with Eliza? He wasn't joking with her when he said he was all in, and now he was terrified. His own feelings made absolutely no sense. Entering the mechanic shop, he saw Daisy, Pie, Bertie, and Landon working in the main garage. They had several cars hooked up, and were doing several different jobs.

"You okay, man?" Landon asked when he walked in.

"Yeah, why?"

"You look a little ... weird. Kind of like a serial killer."

"I'm good."

"Great. Did you know Duke is due back today?"

"Yeah, I did. Did you speak to Maya?"

"I did. She's willing to drop everything so long as she can stay in Vale Valley and never go back to that kind of life. I'll take care of her. It doesn't have to be on club terms or shit like that. I like having her around, and no, it's not because I'm some kind of fucking perv either. I like my women to be, you know, women, legal, and ready to take my cock without complaint."

"I don't need to hear shit about your dick, Landon," Pie said, sliding out from underneath the hood of the car.

"No one believes you're a perv," Bertie said.

"I think I'm in love with Eliza," Brass said, speaking up.

Silence fell on the whole shop as he spoke.

"Like love love, or love love love?" Landon asked.

Brass frowned. "What is the fucking difference?"

"Do you love her like you would a dog, or do you love her like a woman, a wife, and old lady?"

"An old lady." He didn't even hesitate. "She knows about that as well. I told her while we were gone."

"You're meant to keep that shit under wraps until you know for sure," Daisy said.

"I know. I know without a doubt what I feel for her." The more he was around his brothers, the clearer his mind became. "I have no doubts."

"What about her? Does she have doubts?" Daisy asked.

"I don't know."

"You've got to be careful. We all know you got Raoul to get some info on her dad and her soon to be husband."

"She's not marrying him. She wants to be with me as much as I want her. She's going to be my old lady."

He looked at each of the men, and saw the doubt within their gaze.

"What the fuck is it?" he asked.

Daisy sighed, and when no one else spoke up, he took it on himself to be the voice of reason. "How do you know she's not just using you for a quick break away from Daddy?"

"Eliza is not like that."

Daisy shrugged. "I'm watching out for you, and I'm watching out for us and the club. You've got to be with her a lot longer than a handful of weeks to know what you really want. Look at Holly and Duke. They were bouncing around each other for fucking years. Mary and Pike the same. Even Raoul and Zoe."

He couldn't deny that each couple had a lot longer together before they made that final leap to be together.

"What do you want?" Pie asked. "At the end of the day, we can say and do what we want. As brothers we'll be at your side through thick and thin. You know that. We don't want to see you hurt. I don't want to see you hurt."

They were a team. Their decisions were made as one, which was why they all agreed for their old ladies to be taken in such a way. When he first heard it many years ago, he'd figured it was just a way for a bunch of men to get their kicks. Experiencing it the number of times he had, he saw it for something more, something sacred. The idea scared many, aroused plenty, but to the Trojans MC, it was a mark of respect, of unity, and of loyalty. Anyone stepping out on a brother was going to get hurt.

"I'll take my time," he said, seeing the value in waiting.

"With everything going on, I don't want you to jump in, and get burned."

Brass could see why his brothers were so concerned, and he wasn't in the best of minds at the moment either. His feelings for Eliza were all over the place. "Thanks, man."

"You do care about her though, don't you?"

"Yeah, I do." He wasn't in any doubt that he had feelings about her.

****

Eliza was going crazy sitting at home all day writing. Yes, she loved doing it, but the way that Brass just stormed out really pissed her off, and grated on her last nerve. Staring at the screen, the words blended together.

"Screw it." Turning off the computer, she grabbed her jacket, and made her way outside of his home. She went straight toward Mary's house, not sure if she would be there or not. When no one answered, she decided to head toward the diner for some food. She wasn't hungry but the food would offer her comfort, and right now, she needed that. Entering the busy diner, she saw a large man standing at the counter. She wasn't interested in eating at a booth, so she sat in the only available seat near the main desk. The food smelled amazing, and her stomach started to crumble.

"What can I get for you, sweetheart?" he asked.

"I'll take a really strong black coffee, and then whatever you have that is awesome here."

"We have the juiciest, meatiest, cheesiest burger going."

"Then I will have that, and don't forget some apple pie for dessert. I want to eat." She wanted to drown her sorrows in the food that was supplied here, and she didn't care how miserable that made her sound. It was what was going to happen.

"You that posh woman everyone is talking about? The one that is shacking up with Brass?" he asked.

"Wow, news really travels fast around these parts, huh?" she asked.

"It's Vale Valley, and in case you didn't know,

Trojans MC are the shit. Everyone wants to be them, and they're pretty respected around these parts."

"I'm with Brass, but I don't know if I'm *with* him with him." How old was she? She didn't get it. Never had she experienced this amount of indecision. She blew out a breath, and ran fingers through her hair. "Just ignore me."

"The name's Mac, by the way. I own this place."

"Eliza." She shook his hand.

"Nice to meet you. Just so you know, we all have a story to tell in these parts, so you're not weird or different."

"Oh yeah, what's your story?" she asked as he placed her coffee in front of her.

"I saw you with Mary the other day. Pike's woman."

"I know her. She's great."

Mac sighed. "She also used to be part owner in this establishment, and I wanted her for myself. Had hoped that I would win her over in time. I'm not part of the Trojans MC, could be, but decided not to."

He didn't puff his chest out, or try to make out he was better than anyone else.

"Wow."

"Yeah. Anyway, even if I wanted to join the club now, they probably would laugh at me, and Pike would use any excuse to kill me now. No one tries to steal a Trojan's old lady. I don't blame him either. I was a total asshole."

"Burger up," someone said.

Mac grabbed the plate and put it in front of her. "Eat, enjoy, and remember, food is not always the answer, but it certainly helps."

She watched him walk away, and stared down at the juicy burger. Diets had been her whole life, and she'd always seen food like this as a guilty pleasure.

"Fuck it." She grabbed the burger, and took a large bite, closing her eyes, and moaning. Now that was a juicy piece of meat, and so damn tasty. She took another bite, and kept her eyes closed. This way she didn't have to look at anyone, or care that she was eating something so damn good.

Savoring every delicious bite, she made a deal with herself to do no more diets, and just enjoy good food.

"It looks like you're making love to that thing," a woman said.

Eliza's peace was gone, and when she opened her eyes, she turned to see a young girl, dressed in a waitressing uniform with a name badge saying her name was Luna.

"It's really good," she said.

"It always is," Luna said, taking a seat. "I've just finished my morning shift. I can sit here, right?"

"Yes, of course. Go ahead."

"Thanks. My feet are hurting me."

Mac placed a large milkshake in front of Luna, and left them alone.

"They do good shakes, too," Luna said. "You know what, most of the menu was written by Mary and Holly, so you're pretty much good to eat everything."

"Oh." She glanced over at Mac, and wondered if he loved Mary, or if it was just for the good of the restaurant. "Does he love her?" she asked.

Luna didn't even pretend to look confused. "That's what everyone is curious about. Mary is so sweet, and she's feisty as well. No one saw Pike and Mary ever being together because of his rep with the Trojans."

Eliza frowned. "What rep?"

"Oh, you know, Trojans are horn-dogs. They have women who literally sleep with every single one of them.

Not just that, but the horn-dogness goes into their kids as well." Luna blushed. "Anyway, Mary always worked here, and of course you had her blog with Holly, and she helped shape the menus here. She always looked happy, so I think everyone expected her to actually date and marry Mac." Luna shrugged. "I don't think it was ever meant to be. If you ever get the chance, watch the way that Pike watches Mary. He's completely in love with her. It kind of verges on obsession, but that's not a totally bad thing, right?"

"You sound envious."

"I am a little." She sighed. "Okay, I am a lot. I read a lot. I used to go to college and not dwell on everything I don't have, but now all I seem to do is think, you know? Daydream probably. It's what I'm good at." She rested her chin on her palm. "I hate my head sometimes."

Eliza chuckled. "Is there a special guy out there for you?"

"I don't know. There was only one guy for me, and he was kind of an asshole." Luna looked around the diner, and then back at her. "It was with a guy at school. We had sex, and it kind of went too far if you know what I mean. We thought I might be pregnant. Anyway, I wasn't, and I was happy and sad about that. I'll never get to be with him again, and I don't want to be with him again."

She saw the younger girl was torn. "You wanted him, but you didn't want the excess crap that went with him."

"Exactly, and the thing is, he's full of a lot of crap. I don't want to fall for it, and be brokenhearted again. He went from me to another girl, and then I missed my period, and before I knew what was happening, there was this risk that I could trap him. Let's not forget he's also the son of the President of the Trojans. That's just bad news."

That news surprised her.

"You got it bad for a bad boy?" Eliza asked.

"Yeah, I do. I have no idea why I'm telling you all this," Luna said.

"I have one of those faces. It's kindness, and somewhat depressing, and stuff."

Luna chuckled. "I don't even tell my parents about this stuff. They would have a fit if they knew what had happened in my life." She sighed once again.

"Hey, my dad wants me to marry a guy who is in love with another guy, and I'm just to have kids, and be completely miserable."

"Is that why you're still here in Vale Valley?"

"Pretty much, and I really like Brass."

Luna stared at her. "Brass is a good guy. Weird at times, but he fixed my mom's car real good, and only charged her like half of the quote. My mom thought it was some discount, but it wasn't. He's a good guy, and he tries to have this real evil persona, we all know it's fake."

Eliza smiled. "I know." That was why she stuck around, not because of the sex. She enjoyed being with him.

"Does this mean you're going to be his old lady?" Luna asked. "So wrong, 'old lady'."

She wrinkled her nose. "I don't agree with the term either."

"It's wrong. So wrong," Luna said.

"I don't know what I'm going to be." She didn't tell Luna that there was a catch to being with a Trojan.

Luna sipped at her milkshake while Eliza finished her burger.

"Brass is a good guy. You shouldn't be worried

about him at all."

"I'm not."

She watched as Luna finished her shake, did a few stretches, and then got back to work. After she'd eaten her food, she handed some money and a huge tip to Mac, and made her way back toward Brass's home. He still wasn't back, and even though she was a little worried about that, she decided not to dwell too much. Both of them had lives before either of them had actually met. Hers was crap, but his was full of the club, and she was determined not to be one of those women that stalked their boyfriends, and demanded all kinds of crap. That wasn't her.

Chapter Eight

Later that night Brass sat at the bar, and was just finishing up his beer ready to go home. Duke wasn't going to make it home tonight. Their car had broken down, so they had booked into a hotel. Tomorrow Brass and several of his brothers would head out, and go to collect them. They would take their tow truck with them so that Duke didn't have to rely on anyone else to deal with his car. There was only so much trust all of them placed in other people.

"I spoke to Maya. She's going to take the deal if Duke's secured it that is," Landon said, dropping down in the seat next to him.

"Shouldn't you be guarding her?" he asked.

"I am. I'm getting Zoe to look after her for the night. I need a full night's sleep, and she doesn't exactly offer me any reprieve."

"You do look like shit."

"This coming from the guy whose girl was seen eating by herself at Mac's diner, talking with Mac himself."

Brass tensed up, and turned toward him. "What?"

"You didn't hear? It has been all over town, all that anyone can talk about. Brass's woman eating alone. Besides, I'm your designated driver for tonight. I get to make sure your ass is safe at home before I go and camp out for the night."

"We work you to the bone, don't we?" Brass said, spilling sarcasm into his voice.

"It takes a lot to make me look this pretty."

"You're fucking ugly," Pike said. "Not pretty."

"Do I need to be worried about Mac around Eliza?" Brass asked. He watched as Pike tensed.

"I don't know. Mac's a good guy."

"Even though he was hoping to score with your old lady?" Landon asked.

Pike shot the other brother some daggers to which Landon held his hands up.

"I'm only saying the truth. Mac wanted Mary, and let's face it, once you take him out of that stained cover thingy he wears, he's not a bad looking guy," Landon said.

"Really? I'll arrange a date for the two of you, and you can smooch up to the guy."

"He makes a good burger. I could do worse." Landon flung his head back and batted his eyes.

Brass burst out laughing. He had seen Landon balls deep inside one club whore, while fingering another, and licking another's pussy. There is no way Landon was interested in any cock unless it was his own, and it was getting well and truly sucked.

"You guys are fucking killing me here," Brass said.

"I don't think you've got anything to worry about when it comes to Mac, unless he's after your woman, and I don't even know if he was after Mary, or her cooking and recipes. The burger he makes, it's Mary's recipe." Pike sighed.

"You still boycotting the place?" Brass asked.

Pike nodded. The whole Trojans MC were boycotting the diner. None of them had eaten there for a long time.

"I'm worried that if I see him face to face, I'm going to beat the shit out of him, and that is not good for business. Don't want to get locked up, and especially now."

"Why? What's happening now?" Landon asked.

Pike paused. "Nothing. Forget about it."

Before either of them could question him further,

Pike walked away.

"Well that was interesting."

Brass watched Pike's retreating back. "Do you think we're all turning into a bunch of pussies nowadays?"

"How do you mean?"

"There's no parties—"

"Duke has banned parties, remember?" Landon said, interrupting him.

"I know, but look at the club whores. They looked bored." Not to mention that several girls had left as well.

"It's out with the old and in with the new. Some things just change, Brass. I don't think we're getting pussies. I think it's cold, and no one wants to dress in skimpy clothing, and party. I'm never settling down."

"You're not?"

"Nope. I like my pussy with variety. No one bitch is keeping me in place."

Brass chuckled. He finished off his beer, and stood. "Come on then. Let's get out of here."

He had a woman at home, and he needed to make sure she understood exactly who she belonged to.

Landon had his car outside, and he climbed in, strapping the seatbelt.

"I will protect Maya to the death," Landon said. "I'll never accept a deal where we hand her over."

Brass turned toward Landon, who had started up the car and was making his way into town. "No one will ever make that kind of a deal, Landon. You don't need to worry about that shit."

"We shouldn't have to make any kind of deals, and yet we are doing that. It fucking sucks."

He rubbed at his temples. The Abelli situation was a huge problem. He knew that, and it was causing the whole club a headache. They were not used to being given ultimatums and shit. They were hard core bikers. They were not abusers, and beating the shit out of children, which was exactly what Maya was, a child, was not part of the deal. None of them wanted anything to do with that shit.

Duke had killed his ex-wife, but that was because of what she did to Holly and Matthew.

That shit was over.

"Sometimes we need to make concessions and deals like this. Duke will never make a deal he doesn't agree with. It's not who he is," Brass said. "Why don't you have a little faith in the club that you worked your ass off for? We're all going to band together with this shit. It's not about separating. It never was."

Landon nodded. "You're right. Shit, I've not had a lot of sleep, and I'm clearly not thinking well."

"Good." They pulled up outside of Brass's home. "Go home, text me when you get there, and get some fucking sleep. That is a damn order."

Climbing out of the car, he headed inside seeing only a few lights on. Entering the house, he was overcome with the smell of burning. Following the smell, he found Eliza in the kitchen, glaring at a mixing bowl.

He cleared his throat, and she looked up. "I think I burnt the chocolate. It's all gritty, and that smell is horrible."

Brass moved toward the bowl, and took a small sniff. "Yep, it's completely burnt."

"I'll toss it out and start again."

She ignored him, throwing the mixture into the trash before moving toward the sink. He saw her laptop was set up on the counter. Brass was an idiot, and knew she was giving him the silent treatment.

"I heard you had lunch today at Mac's diner."

"Yep."

"None of the Trojans go there."

"Fine."

"We're all there for Pike. I don't know if you know, but Mac was after Mary, and we're all—"

"I know."

Again, she didn't look up, nor did she pay him any attention.

Her long raven hair was pulled back into a ponytail, and she was reading from her computer.

"It was a long day. How was yours?" he asked.

"Fine."

"Eliza?"

"What?"

"Look at me."

He heard her sigh, and then lift her head. The shirt she wore was much too big, and spilled over one shoulder, showing off a white bra strap. She also wore a pair of jeans. The shirt was so big that it hid the view of her ass. He loved her ass.

"I'm looking."

"What's the problem?" he asked.

"You want to know what the problem is?" she asked, leaning on the counter, and staring right at him. Her green eyes blazed fire, all of it coming his way. It only served to enflame his cock.

"Yeah, I do. I wouldn't ask."

"What was your fucking problem this morning?" she asked.

If she was cussing, he knew he was in fucking trouble. "What do you mean?"

"Don't give me that." She slammed her hand against the counter. "God, I told you I liked you, and then you went a little crazy on me. You just ... changed. What did I say or do that was wrong?"

"Nothing."

"Nothing? Then why did you run out of here as if you were being chased by a pack of savage wolves, huh?" she asked.

"Why did you go to Mac's to eat?" he asked, moving closer to her.

"I was hungry, and I wanted some food. His place looked pretty damn good."

"Yeah, well he has a reputation for trying to steal what doesn't belong to him."

"So now I belong to you, is that it?" she asked.

"Yeah."

"What was your problem this morning? Did I say the wrong thing?" she asked.

"No."

"If all it means is that whenever you don't like something you can just disappear, that's not going to work for me. That will never work for me."

"I didn't say it was."

"Then what the hell?" she asked. She took a step toward him so that they were now standing toe to toe. "What is your problem?"

Brass didn't know what to say. He felt like an asshole, and he was behaving like one, but she didn't make it easy for him either. He wanted everything with her, and yet she seemed to be able to keep her shit together, even if she just stayed silent. What happened to women that were easy to read? Eliza, she was confusing as fuck.

"This is my problem!" He sank his fingers into her hair, and pulled her close. Slamming his lips down on hers, he silenced any and all protest. He didn't want to hear any more shit coming out of her mouth. Plunging his tongue inside, he felt her slowly begin to melt against him.

This was the one area that they matched. Pressing

her up against the counter, he ran his hands all over her body.

"We shouldn't be doing this."

"We're fucking doing this," he said. She had finished her cycle yesterday, and now he was going to taste her pretty cunt.

Tugging on the shirt, he tore it from her body, and threw it to the floor.

"I liked that shirt."

"It was fucking ugly. Anything that covers up these beauties needs to be destroyed." He cupped her tits together, and pulled her bra down, exposing her nipples. Flicking his tongue against each bud, he relished her moans.

He moved her out of the way, slid his hand across the counter, shoving everything to the floor. Several items smashed, and he ignored them. He'd deal with the cleanup later. All he wanted was his woman, naked, and ready for him.

"Brass," she said.

He lifted her up and started to tug on her jeans. She used her hands, lifting her body up so that he could slide her jeans down her thighs, and throw them to the floor as well. Her panties followed, and then he had her legs spread. As he slid a finger inside her wet cunt, they both groaned.

"This belongs to me, Eliza. You're mine whether you like it or not. All mine. All fucking mine." He would say the words all day if she had to hear them. Kissing her tits one at a time, he glided his tongue down her body, dipping into her bellybutton, and then going further down to between her thighs. Spreading her open, he licked her clit, circling the bud.

"Oh, Brass, that feels so good."

It was about to get a whole lot better. With his

hand, he pushed her down so that she was lying completely flat on the counter. He pulled her toward the edge using her hips, and forced her to spread her thighs even wider.

The lips of her sex parted, and he took a second to admire her juicy pussy. Sliding a finger inside her cunt, he watched her suck him up. Adding a second finger, he didn't look away, not once, knowing his cock was going to be inside her, balls deep.

"Who do you belong to?" he asked.

"You, Brass. Only you."

"That's right. This pussy is mine. Every part of you belongs to me, and I'm never going to give you up. You're going to belong to me. Every single part of you." Leaning down, he continued to fuck her with his fingers, only this time, he sucked her clit into his mouth.

Her pussy tightened around him, and her fingers sank into his hair. She was writhing on his tongue and fucking herself on his fingers. He felt her pussy start to pulse and contract. Within seconds she screamed his name, riding her orgasm on his fingers. He didn't give her a chance to come down from the peak. Sliding his jeans off, he picked her up, and carried her through to the sitting room. Bending her over the chair, he found her entrance, and slammed every single inch of his dick inside her.

They both cried out, and Brass didn't give a shit that he wasn't wearing a condom. This thing between them was happening. He wasn't about to walk away, and no matter what Pie or any of his other club brothers said, this was the real fucking deal, and as such, he was going to make Eliza his woman. She was perfect for him, and had a place within the club.

He'd make it so.

Wrapping her hair around his hand, he started to

pound inside her, watching his cock slide in and out of her, covered in her cum.

"You belong to me. You're mine."

Each word, he drove home with the thrust of his cock. From the moment she broke down in Vale Valley, she had belonged to him, and he wasn't giving her up.

****

Eliza stared up at the ceiling mirror. They had fucked three times already, and her body was sore, spent, sated. Brass was lying beside her with their feet where the pillows should be.

"Do you really like watching yourself?" she asked.

"Yeah. It's not always me I'm watching, babe. It's you as well."

"You're a watcher."

He took hold of her hand, locking their fingers together. She should be covering up her body. Next to him, all of her imperfections were blaringly obvious. Her stomach was too rounded. There was no gap between her thighs. There were some dots of cellulite, and there was lumps and bumps all over the place.

Brass, he was perfection. Hard abs, solid muscles, ink all over the place. She looked like an advert for diet pills. He looked like an advert for the gym.

"I don't want you eating at Mac's," he said.

"I know what happened between him and Mary. I don't exactly know the full details but I do get it, and I do understand. I'd never step out on you. If you don't want me to eat at Mac's, I won't." She turned to look at him rather than at his reflection. "I know I was engaged to be married to another man when I met you, but I never wanted that. I never felt attracted or even wanted to marry him. I still don't, Brass. I meant what I said when I told you I would be in this for real." She squeezed his hand.

"It's not just that. We're all with Pike on this one."

"I like Luna," she said. "We got talking today."

"Matthew's Luna."

"Is that what she is?"

"Duke's kid. His eldest is called Matthew."

"Pregnancy scare?" she asked.

"The very one."

"I like her. We got talking today."

"Eliza?"

"Yeah."

"I want you to be my old lady. For real, in front of the club." He cupped her cheek. "I want us to be together like that, completely."

Her heart was pounding. "I want to be with you as well. I don't know if I'm ready to do what you need me to do."

"Not right away. There are no parties at the club right now, and with everything going on, I don't want to add us to the mix. One day, I want you to be my old lady in more than words. I want the club to know that you're mine."

She couldn't help it. Tears sprang to her eyes, and she smiled at him. "I'm so sorry. I promised myself that I wouldn't cry, and here I go, crying."

"Your tears are beautiful." He moved her hand out of the way, and kissed her lips.

Placing a hand on his chest, she halted him.

"What is it?" he asked.

"I, erm …" Her cheeks were heating and she hadn't even gotten to the best part yet. "I may not be ready for the old lady club thing yet, but there's something else I'm ready for."

"Oh yeah?"

She nodded, pressing a kiss to his lips. "I want you to be my first."

"First what?"

"You're just teasing me right now so that I will say it, right?"

He laughed. "I'm such an innocent guy, Eliza. I need you to say the words for exactly what it is that you want."

She sighed. "Fine. Fine. Brass, I want you to fuck my ass." She kissed him so that he wouldn't say another word.

"I always knew you would come around to my way of thinking." He ran his hand down her side, moving behind to grab her ass.

"Do you think you can do it tonight?" she asked.

"I have all the stuff," he said. "I wanted to own every single part of you, Eliza. Ever part. Every hole. Including this one."

She was nervous, but it was so damn sexy, and hot. "Then I'm putting myself in your capable hands, Brass." She rolled so that she was on her stomach. "How do you want me?"

Brass pressed a kiss to the back of her neck, making her shiver. "Stay exactly as you are. That is perfect."

She watched him climb off the bed and disappear toward his bathroom. This wasn't just a quick decision for her. She had been thinking about it for a very long time. A lot longer than he'd even been asking. Anal sex had always intrigued her, and she wanted it so badly now with Brass.

He came back with a tube of lube and a large dildo. "I'm going to start stretching you with this." He moved not he bed behind her, straddling her legs.

She pressed her head to her hands, and waited.

EASY

Brass pressed a pillow beneath her, lifting her up, and then his hands spread open the cheeks of her sex. His fingers slid into her pussy, drawing them back, and coating her anus. She released a little squeal as the lubrication gel was so cold on her body.

"Sorry, babe." He coated her asshole with the gel, and she tensed up as he started to press a finger inside her. It was almost too much, and then it wasn't enough, and she couldn't stop her body from tensing up.

It was as if he sensed that, and with his other hand, he slid it between her thighs, stroking her clit.

She found herself relaxing, opening her thighs wider for his cock, desperate for him to go deeper inside her.

The finger at her ass slowly slid inside her to the knuckle. It was almost too full, and at the same time not enough. The pleasure and bite of pain drew together, confusing every single one of her senses. She didn't know where he started, or where she did. Nothing made sense in her world.

He added a second finger and started to stretch her ass. She released a whimper but not for him to stop. She wanted more. She wanted his cock inside her pussy and ass.

"You want this, don't you, babe?" he asked.

She nodded. "Yes, yes, I do." She hadn't realized exactly how much until he started teasing her body, drawing pleasure from it that she hadn't expected.

When he added a third finger, and she was able to take that without any complaints, he removed his fingers, and replaced them with the dildo. That was bigger and thicker than his fingers. He used plenty of lube as it slid inside her with such ease.

"You're so wet," he said, and she was.

Eliza had never been so aroused in her life. The

pleasure, the pain, the sensations were all consuming, driving her to press against the cock inside her ass.

He wasn't done. When she began to fuck the cock inside her, he removed that, and then his cock was pressing to her anus.

His cock was far bigger than his fingers and the dildo he used.

Inch by inch, he slid inside her, giving her the chance to accommodate his cock. He filled her up, blowing her world, and making her awaken to needs that she had thought were long dead.

"Your ass is so tight, baby. So tight, and so fucking hot."

She cried out as he slid the last inch inside her, finally full to the brim. "You've got it all, baby. It's all inside you."

He pressed kisses to the back of her neck, moving from each side, giving her time to get used to his cock in her ass. She loved his touch, and when she couldn't stand to wait any longer, she started to push back against him, making him ride her ass. He gripped her hips, and began to withdraw from her ass. With only the tip of him inside her, she cried out, wanting more of him. Slowly, Brass began to fuck her ass, taking his time, and drawing out every single cry, beg, and whimper that she had to possess.

She was a complete and total goner for this man. There was no holding back now. Only moving forward.

Chapter Nine

The instant Duke got back to the clubhouse he demanded an all church meeting. This was a little different though. This had several of the club ladies involved, Maya, along with Russ and Sheila. What was also a big surprise was Clinton Briar's presence. He was the lawyer that had brought the shit-storm of Abelli to their front door.

Brass sat in his usual chair, feeling like the room was a little overcrowded.

"You all know that I went to see Francis Abelli the day before last. He's Holly's grandfather, and still remaining head of the Abelli mafia. They are deadly, and they are dangerous. He promises to keep Anton in line with three promises from us. The first, he wants us to be his muscle, to help him when he needs. It won't be every single weekend, but he wants an alliance with us. The Trojans MC at his back, and he'll pay us as well. This is an extension of a business relationship. Second, he wants to get to know Holly and our kids. He also wants to know you, Maya. He says that he hasn't seen enough of you, and that he is deeply sorry over what happened to you."

Brass glanced over at Maya to see her cheeks were red.

"What's the third promise?" Russ asked.

"That Maya is not testify against the Abelli name. If she agrees to do that, then he will extend his protection to the club and the town. Nothing will come of it, and he will personally see to the punishment of Anton."

"No, you just wait one fucking minute," Clinton said. "This man is a criminal. She's not doing it."

"I agree to those terms," Maya said.

Brass looked at Landon. His jaw was tense, showing he was pretty pissed off at the deal.

"Maya, you do that and they will arrest you, and have you locked up," Clinton said.

"No, they won't," Landon said, looking toward Duke. "He's got his hands everywhere. Maya will simply disappear, right?"

"That's right. She can stay here, or wherever you decide you want to go. Maya, there will be protection for you."

"I like Vale Valley. I like being here, and I would love to help you guys with everything. It's the least I can do for what I've done to you."

"You've not done anything wrong," Clinton said. "This, what you're doing, backing away, that is wrong."

"I know you want me to testify, but if I even make it to court, they are going to tear me apart, Clinton."

"I can protect you," Clinton said.

"Really? You can promise me that they won't put in a few jibes, or have some kind of evidence that makes it look like I wanted it?" she asked. "All they need is to give doubt. That's all. Doubt, and everyone walks."

Clinton sighed and dropped his arms down.

"You didn't just bring in one girl to take down an army, Clinton," Duke said. "We're an entire club, and against the Abellis some of us would die, but not all. You're talking an all out war that quite frankly you're not even ready for. You will not guilt this girl into doing what you want." Duke looked toward Maya. "I will not guilt you into doing anything. This decision is on you, and I told Francis you will need time. I will give that to you. Think it over, and come back to me."

"I don't need time to think it over. If Granddad has said that, then I know we're all protected. It's my father that's a complete nut job. If Granddad can keep him in line, we're all safe." She locked her hands together, and stayed in her seat. Her gaze was on her lap.

Brass saw everyone was a little shaken.

"Are you just going to take orders from this man?" Clinton asked, looking at Duke.

"I don't take orders from anyone." Duke glared right back at the lawyer. Every single man had tensed in the room.

"You are. This man tells you to do shit, you're doing it. He's a fucking criminal—"

Duke stood up, his chair scraping along the floor before falling with a clatter. "Then what the fuck am I? I make deals that mean this club is looked after. I do the shit that keeps this town fucking clean. I don't sit around on my ass all day spewing out rules and order from some fucking book that pussies have created. You want to take me on, fine, take me on, Clinton. You wanted to bring Abelli to his fucking knees, fine. Did you even give a shit about what he did to Maya, or is this just one big case?" His questions filled the air, and they all knew the answers. "Everyone always looks to us as the wrongdoers here. We don't follow the rules, we do shit our way. We have our own code. The real crooks are you fuckers. The law, the ones that can be bent with the right price."

"That's not fucking true."

"You went after Abelli with a teenage girl as fucking evidence. The same girl you couldn't protect and who was gang raped, and beaten near to fucking death. Then you come into my home, and ask for my help. I'm giving you my help right now because Holly belongs to me, and that is my only connection to this shit! They are my men, and Maya is under my protection. I did what was right by my club, my woman, and my fucking family. Don't you fucking dare disrespect me again— otherwise you'll be following everyone else who thought they could challenge me."

Silence hung in the air.

"It's time for you to go," Holly said, grabbing Clinton, and urging him out of the room.

Duke sat down. His shoulders on the desk, and he was staring at Maya. "You're family as well. I will do whatever it takes to protect you, and to protect this club."

"Thank you. I'll take the deal. I don't need to think about it."

"You will always have a home here."

Maya nodded and then left the room. The women all turned to leave until there were only the men left.

"Was it bad?" Pike asked, taking a seat now that his woman was gone.

"It wasn't bad. Francis Abelli is in charge, and he knows what he is doing for the most part. The biggest problem is Anton Abelli. Francis believes that he can punish his son, keep him under control," Duke said.

"You don't think that's true?" Brass asked.

"He didn't even know the extent of Maya's injuries. I'm not convinced that anyone can keep Anton in check unless Anton is killed."

"Then kill him," Russ said.

Duke slammed his palm down on the table, and glared at Russ. "Your chance to tell me what to do passed a long time ago, old man. This is your shit-storm, and I'm cleaning it up. You want to die, go and kill him. I'll make sure to throw your ashes down the toilet with a nice big pile of shit."

Brass looked at Duke and then at Russ. This was the first time that the two men had ever spoken out against each other. Russ was once the President, and now Duke ruled. This could turn ugly.

The standoff ended with Russ leaving, and Duke snarled. "There will be no parties, no wild behavior, and no alcohol taken until further notice. I need you all to be on your best, and your guard. I will not lose a man for this fucking shit. I know some of you will be pissed about this decision. I really don't give a shit. You want to stay alive, do as I say. You don't, put your cut down on the table, and walk out of the fucking door."

No one handed over their cut.

"Dismissed."

Leaving the clubhouse room, he saw Holly was waiting outside.

Brass made his way outside to have a smoke. His time at the Trojans had been filled with threats, partying, and sex. This was one of those times it was filled with threats.

"Some hardcore shit. Don't ever recall Duke going that crazy," Pie said, moving to stand in front of him.

"Shit is about to get real fucking mean." Brass took a deep suck on his cigarette. "We all need to be ready."

"He's pissed off. Duke's never like that, and especially not with Russ. He's feeling betrayed."

"You think you understand feelings now?" Brass asked.

"Think about it. The club was part of Russ. It's part of all of us, and the same goes with Duke. When you hand it over, you hand it over with all of its secrets. This secret is twenty years old, and it finally coming to bite someone on the ass. Wouldn't you feel a little betrayed?"

"Yeah, I fucking would." Brass took another drag on his cigarette and watched as Russ and Sheila were talking.

They were all paying for the mistakes of those two, and it was getting old real fucking fast.

"Maya's strong though," Brass said. "I didn't expect her to take that kind of a deal."

"She wants to live her life. I can't blame her. I'm

heading out. Catch you later."

****

"What does it mean?" Eliza asked, then took a sip of her wine. She had made pasta for when Brass had returned home.

Club meetings were really important, almost sacred. They had been in the middle of having sex when the club had called, telling him there was a church meeting. He'd had no choice but to go, leaving her soaking wet, and desperate for his cock all day long.

"It means we've got to stay on our guard. We're not having any more trips to the beach for a long time."

"That's fine. I can wait." She smiled, sipping at her wine. "I'm sorry about all this mess you're dealing with."

"It's club business. Until you're taken as my old lady, I can't take you into those meetings."

"It's fine, Brass." She twirled her fork in the spaghetti and started to chew, watching him. He was clearly worried, and she hated that. She wished there was something she could say or do that would help him. "Mary called. She invited me to the first barbeque of the season. I don't know when it is, but she said it is a huge deal at the clubhouse and as your plus one she was going to invite me."

"That's great." He sipped at his beer.

Putting down her fork, she got up, and moved toward him. There was enough space, so she straddled his legs and wrapped her arms around his neck. Teasing the fine hairs at the base, she stared into his eyes, knowing that she would do anything that would make him feel so good.

"What are you doing?" he asked, both of his hands grabbing her ass.

"This morning, we were interrupted. I think it's

only fair that we make up for what we didn't get to finish." She bit on his earlobe, sucking it into her mouth, giggling as he growled. "And I've been thinking about you all day long. I need you, Brass." She began to move over his rock hard dick, moaning as he seemed to touch the right spot.

His hands held onto her ass tightly. She kissed from his neck, up, taking his lips, and biting down onto his lip. "You've got a lot of fire inside you," he said.

"And it is all for you." Sliding her tongue across his bottom lip, she took charge, deepening the kiss as he worked her shirt off. This time he didn't go to destroy it, which she was thankful for.

"You're going to drive me crazy."

"That's the idea." She wanted him crazy for her. Pulling away, she finished removing the shirt from her body, and stood up. As he took care of his jeans, she removed the few items of clothing so that she was completely naked.

He held his cock up, and she straddled his legs, sinking onto his large cock. The moment he was inside her, she felt complete, whole. "I missed you today," she said.

"I missed you, too."

He held onto the cheeks of her ass and started to lift her up and down his cock. Her tits bounced with each downward thrust, and she took his lips. Brass cried out and held her with him thrust up to the hilt inside her.

Pulling away from his lips, she leaned back to stare at him.

"Damn, I want this every single fucking day. I want to be balls deep inside your pussy."

"Or my ass," she said.

"You liked that, babe?" he asked. "You liked me being inside your juicy ass."

"Yes, I did. I want it so much."

He grabbed her ass and started to fuck inside her. This was where their relationship started, but it was so much more now. The feelings she felt for Brass were real, true, and pure. She wouldn't let him go, nor would she allow her father to destroy what she had come to love.

Love Brass, she did, and she would fight every single person who tried to hurt him, or the club.

****

Matthew stared at Luna, and damn it, even in the rain she looked so beautiful. "Did you walk here?" he asked.

"I had nothing better to do. What is this?" she asked, holding up a single letter. His father had arranged for Luna's college to be paid in full.

"What is what?" he asked.

"Don't give me that. I've done some research, and the company that apparently is investing in my career happens to reside in Vale Valley. It's you, isn't it?" she asked. "Don't lie to me, Matthew. Just tell me the truth."

The rain was coming down thick and fast. "Yeah, it's true. I got my dad to agree to help you."

"Why?" she asked. "Is this charity? Do you pity me?"

"Because you deserve it, Luna. You don't deserve to be waiting tables at Mac's fucking diner, or working to all hours of the freaking night. You deserve the chance at something better to get out of town if that is what you want."

She stared at him with her mouth open. "I'm not your responsibility."

"This is not about that. It has never been about that. I want you to have everything, Luna."

He had messed things up between them, but that didn't for a second mean he couldn't look after her.

"I don't need this."

"No, you don't, but tell me, were you not a little happy when you saw it?"

She didn't say a word at first. "I don't know if I can take this."

"Take it. It's yours anyway." He stepped out into the rain, not caring about how cold it was. "Let me do this for you."

"Is this because of what happened our senior year? What we did?" she asked.

"No. It's because of what I didn't do. You're perfect, Luna, and I was an asshole. Being with you, it was the best feeling in the world, and rather than trust it, I went and fucked another girl. I'm not proud of it, and it was the worst moment of my life. I know I lost you. Let me do this for you. Let me take care of you any way I can."

Tears filled her eyes, and she sighed. "I can't, Matthew. It's not right."

"Fuck what is right or not. I owe this to you for breaking your heart." He reached out, cupping her cheek. Just that one touch made him feel so alive. "Please."

She closed her eyes, and leaned a little heavily against him. It wasn't much, but to Matthew it was everything.

"Okay, I'll take this."

****

Duke and Holly watched as Matthew pulled Luna in for a hug.

"I've got a feeling that girl is going to become our daughter-in-law," Duke said.

"You're only just figuring that out."

"You had an idea?"

"Please, you don't forget a condom with a girl unless you're wanting something more," Holly said.

"Or you just want to fuck so badly you don't really care what you catch." Duke moved away from the window. He had seen enough of his son's love life. He didn't need to see anymore.

"That's not what happened with Luna, and you know it. We weren't there, and Matthew has been having sex for a lot longer than even I want to think about," Holly said.

Duke sat on the end of his bed, and held his arms open. "Come here."

She stepped into his arms, smiling. "What are you thinking about?" she asked.

"You and me. Our family. The club. Do you think I'm making the right decision about all this?"

Holly stroked the back of his neck. "Yeah, I do. If Maya had asked for you to take this further then I would have agreed with her. She wants this to end, and you can see that all she really wants out of life is to be safe. We can offer her that."

"Landon looked so pissed. So did Russ."

"I know. We can only do what we have to. What about Clinton? Will he cause a few problems?" she asked.

He sighed. "Probably. I figure we can arrange a barbeque. I've already called Francis and told him we'll take the deal. He'll handle Anton. In a few weeks' time we'll do a barbeque, and then we can talk with Clinton. Francis said he would call with time for us to prepare when he needs us."

"That's what I'm worried about. I don't want anything to happen to you and the club."

"Nothing will, babe. I won't let it. Everything I've done, I've done for the club, and for all of us."

"I know there was nothing to be done. I just wish you didn't have to strike a deal for the club. Does Abelli really have that much reach?" she asked.

"Yeah, he does. Anton, he's a problem. Francis has told me that Russ and Sheila will be safe. Nothing will happen to them. He has given me his word. I wouldn't take any deal unless I could guarantee the outcome, you know that, babe."

"I do." She sighed. "I've heard that Brass wants to claim Eliza as his old lady."

"Yeah, Pie told me that he's asked for the brother to wait to know more."

"You don't think she's good enough for Brass?" she asked.

"I don't know. It hasn't been all that long. She came to Knuckles and Beth's wedding, that's all I know. Oh, and her dad is supposed to be this asshole that pretty much can make our lives a misery."

"Anyone with money can make our lives a misery. Brass is different around Eliza. You can't deny it. He also isn't sleeping with any of the other women, and this is Brass."

"I know." Duke rubbed at his eyes. "A lot to deal with, I know. We'll get through it."

"My big strong biker. You're a good man, and a good leader."

Right then he didn't feel like it.

SAM CRESCENT

Chapter Ten

One week later

Brass was finishing up his write up on the car he had just finished working on. Next week he would finally take Eliza as his old lady, and he already had the evening planned out. First, he was going to make love to her at home, and then they would head out to the barbeque that Holly and Mary had been organizing. They'd mingle, have some food, ready for him to take her. Maybe a few drinks to help her a little bit.

"You're off in dream land," Bertie said, coming to stand beside him.

"I've got the love of a good woman." He smiled. Eliza had told him last night that she loved him. It had been faint, and she had looked really embarrassed about it. Of course when he told her that he felt the same, she hadn't believed him. Weird woman.

All women want was for their men to tell them how much they love them. The first time he does, and what happens, she doesn't believe him.

"It's love now?" Bertie asked.

"Yeah, it is. I love her, and she loves me. Do you need me to draw you a diagram? Will that make you feel better?" he asked.

"Defensive much?" Chip asked.

Brass held his hand up. "Sorry."

"It's Pie's fault," Bertie said. "Pie told him to give it time. To wait and see if she is the right one."

"I know, and when you find a woman of your own, you will know, too."

"There is no chance of that ever happening," Pie said. "I love pussy too much, and the thought of being with one woman all the time, freaks me the fuck out. Monogamy was made up by a bunch of old women designed to keep man under wraps."

"Just remember, you say that about men, and the same rules apply to women," Bertie said. "You find a woman you like banging, and she loves to fuck as well? Guess you will be one in a long line."

Pie shook his head. "I've got a king size cock, my friend. I've got women panting after me."

"And that's why you're going to be the one to get burned," Brass said, laughing.

Pie stuck his fingers up at them, telling them all to go and fuck it.

Brass continued to chuckle as he finished up the forms, and took them into the main office where Landon was working. "You okay?"

"Yeah, I'm good."

"You look tired."

"I told you I'm more than fine. It has just been a rough couple of nights with her. Ever since Duke came back from seeing her grandfather. It's like everything has come back into focus in her mind, and she can't seem to get over it. You know?"

"It's a lot to get over. I doubt she will ever really be over it, Landon."

"I know. I just want to help her. She's like the sister I never had."

Brass patted Landon's shoulder, trying to offer the brother comfort. It was really hard to do. "Here, this car is finished and ready to be picked up." He handed over the keys, and headed toward the lot to see whichever car was on his list. Their mechanic shop was always busy, and with winter nearly behind them, everyone was planning for their vacation.

Vacation. He needed to plan somewhere for him and Eliza to go. Somewhere warm that was not overly crowded, but an awesome place to be together, explore.

That was something he needed to think about.

"Excuse me," a gentleman said.

Brass turned along with everyone else in the main garage. The man was wearing a really expensive business suit, gray haired, without a speck of imperfection.

"What can we do for you?" Bertie asked. "You got a flat that needs repairing?"

Brass had a feeling he knew who the guy was.

"I'm here to talk to the man shacking up with my daughter."

Bingo. He was right.

"Sorry, man, that could be anyone around here. You're going to have to be more specific," Chip said.

"Eliza Bishop. I want to speak to the man who thinks he's good enough for the Bishop name."

Wow, this asshole was a piece of work. Good for Brass, he was as well.

"I'm him, and I take it you're Daddy!" He walked with a swagger, moving his hands really far out, and looking a little cocky. He knew how to play the asshole, and this was exactly what the guy was going to get. Daddy Bishop didn't care about his daughter, just the name that she possessed. Staring at the man who had raised Eliza, Brass was starting to understand some of Eliza's quirks.

He'd noticed in the mornings how she always second guessed what she was wearing. There would be a formal black skirt and white blouse that would then change to something different. Even when she wore baggy clothes, she always made sure her hair was made up, and he rarely got to see her ruffled.

Her father looked him up and down. "Let's settle this properly." He pulled out a small rectangular checkbook. "Who should I make this out to?"

"You're not going to buy me."

"Everyone has a price. It's simple. You're not keeping my daughter, and all you have to do is name the price, and I'll be out of your hair, along with my daughter. I'm sure she's done nothing but be a nuisance anyway."

Brass felt his brothers behind his back. They were there for him, and now they saw what Eliza had been dealing with.

"I'm not for sale, and neither is Eliza. She's mine."

"Please, Darcy is over there right now to deal with her. You want a million, I'll pay it. Ten, twenty, just name your price. You'll be a very rich man, and you won't even have to think about this shit."

"You really think I'm a man that can be bought."

Bishop looked around at the mechanic shop, and there was a curl to his lip, disgust clear on his face. "Frankly, yes. Everyone can be purchased, and this is just … pitiful. Even Eliza can do better, and that is saying a lot."

Darcy is over there right now…

Hell no.

Without another word, Brass pushed past Bishop and climbed on his bike. There was no time to wait around. He was going toward his girl, and he was going to make sure that no one hurt her again. She belonged to him, no one else.

****

Eliza laughed at Holly's story of Matthew when he was growing. She never thought a teenage boy could be so much fun, but it seems Matthew was full of tricks.

Mary, Zoe, Leanna, and Holly had all descended on her home. Brass's home that was now her home, and they were making up some cookies for the kids school fair that afternoon. She had never had so much fun with a bunch of women. Not only were they all baking together, and chatting, there was just a feeling of family and togetherness that she had always envied but never gotten the chance to be part of.

"So we heard that Brass is going to make you his old lady," Mary said.

She paused in the measuring of the chocolate chips. Her cheeks heated knowing what each woman had to go through.

"We clearly don't need to worry about giving her a warning. She knows," Holly said. "About how we all became old ladies."

Again her cheeks were burning. "I know. I just, I don't know if that is going to be something I can do. It's so … personal. Being with a guy and then having someone else watch."

"I found it hot, especially as I know that I now belong to Raoul. He's mine, and I'm his. The other stuff is just club details. I get it in a really weird way, I understand it. I just don't always agree to it." Zoe took another cookie off the tray. "What is wrong with me? I throw up in the morning … like all the time, and now I can't drink coffee. I'm so hungry, and these are so good."

Leanna, Mary, and Holly shared a look.

"Sweetie, you're pregnant," Leanna said.

Zoe's eyes went wide. "No, I'm not. We've been trying for ages, and we had a false positive a few months ago, and we got really excited." She placed a hand to her stomach. "No. I would know, wouldn't I?"

"Some women don't know until they are giving birth," Eliza said. "I read it in the paper I think. Or they lied and they knew the whole time."

"I'm telling you, you're pregnant. Raoul's going to have a little boy or girl walking around," Holly said.

"Or both," Mary said. "Twins."

"Hell no. I'm not having twins. Not today, and not ever. No way. There's no way that twins can even be birthed naturally. My vagina couldn't handle something like that," Zoe said.

Eliza winced. Babies were all well and good to think about, but not many thought about the fact that a baby, a real life, large baby was going to come out of something that was quite small in comparison.

Her own vagina tensed up at the thought.

"You'll forget all about the pain," Holly said. "It's—"

"Really painful to start but when they place that little bundle of joy in your arms, you forget, and you want another one like a baby or sister for them," Mary said, touching her own stomach.

"I can't even think about this right now. I don't know if I can think about it and even make sense of what is going to happen to my body," Zoe said.

"First we need to get you a kit. A pregnancy test kit," Eliza said. "I can go to the pharmacy. It's not far from here."

Just then someone knocked at the door.

"I can go after I answer this, and then I can go and get you one," Eliza said.

"Someone will see you."

"That's the point, babe. Brass will have a hissy fit, but I'll tell him the truth, and then you'll have time to tell Raoul. It's perfect, don't you think?" She opened the door, and gasped. There on her doorstep was Darcy, and he didn't look all that inviting.

"Hello, Eliza. Nice of you to finally answer your door."

"Darcy, what the hell are you doing here?" she asked.

At his name the others moved up behind her,

peering at him. He was like a spectacle at the zoo. What the hell was he doing at Brass's front door?

Crap. She hadn't expected this.

She had hoped that her family would just move on and accept that she didn't want to be just another pawn in the Bishop empire. She wanted her own life, and to be with Brass. He was her entire world, and she didn't care if she sounded stupid thinking or believing it. She loved Brass, and there was no way she was ever leaving him.

"I find this all a bit tasteless," Darcy said, looking behind her at the women. "Come on. It's time to go. You can leave everything here, and we're heading out now. Your father is taking care of Brass."

"Not happening," she said.

When he made to grab her, she pulled away. Darcy had never touched her, and she didn't want his touch right now either.

He was a lie.

Her father was a lie.

The life she had before Vale Valley was a lie.

There was no way she was going back there.

No way in hell.

"You're going to be difficult?" Darcy asked.

"My life is here now. I don't want anything to do with you or my father, or the Bishops. You can forget about everything."

"And you ruined a perfectly good moment," Zoe said. "Men!"

"Whatever you were discussing is not of any relevance to me. You know that whoever you're shacking up with will take whatever money your father wants. When are you going to realize that money is better than you?"

His words cut her to the core. Darcy had always had that magical gift of making her feel both small and stupid.

"Who the hell do you think you are?" Holly said. "You think you can buy any of the Trojans? We're made of a lot stronger stuff, believe me."

Someone gripped her arms and pulled her back. Each one of the Trojan old ladies surrounded her.

"Don't you listen to him," Leanna said.

"Brass would never pick money over you. It will never happen."

"I see I didn't get here with enough time," Brass said, appearing behind Darcy. "Don't think the worst of me now, Eliza."

She couldn't help but smile. "They didn't buy you."

"You're worth a lot more than twenty million dollars, baby."

"Twenty million?"

"Yeah, and he only just started negotiations."

"You better get your hands off my fiancée," Darcy said.

"She's not your fiancée, and why don't you marry that guy that you're going to be taking to the marriage bed?" Brass asked.

Darcy went white, and looked toward her. "You would talk about private matters."

"I would talk about anything with my guy. I'm going to be Brass's old lady, which makes me the property of the Trojans MC. I'm not yours to bully anymore. Stay away from me."

She slammed the door in Darcy's face, and turned to Brass. "You told him no."

"I told him no, and, babe, I get it, I really do. Your father is a fucking asshole, and I promise you, you'll always feel treasured and loved in my company." He pressed a kiss to her lips. "Always."

"Ahhh," the women said who had gathered around them.

"Can we have a little bit of privacy right now?" Brass said.

"Yes, yes, we're going somewhere," Zoe said. "May as well get the test, go to the toilet, and call Raoul. Let's get this over with."

Each of the women left the house, and Brass turned toward her. "Test?"

"Zoe thinks she's pregnant. I was going to go and pick up the test to give her time to process everything, and then Darcy was there, and I didn't get the chance. You do love me." She didn't care about anything else.

"Yeah. You've had boyfriends before that have taken the money and run?"

"Yep, you've got it. Some have only gone to take me out for coffee, and run out on me. It has been hard to find a guy who wants me, not the money." He stroked her cheek, and tears filled her eyes. "You want me."

"Always. I told you. From the moment you broke down, and your posh ass was demanding we fix the car."

"It was all a front. I've seen my father and mother like that, and I was scared. I hope I didn't offend you or anyone else."

"You can offend me more often, in stiletto heels, and knowing my cock is going to be deep inside you for the rest of the damn day."

She chuckled. "They won't go away easily."

"They will. I just need to call Raoul to bring Diaz here, and a meeting, and believe me, your father and Darcy will go running away, and you'll be mine."

She wrapped her arms around his neck and pressed a kiss to his lips. She really had found the love of her life.

****

Duke knocked on Matthew's bedroom door. His son was all grown up, and was heading back to college. He couldn't see a reason to keep him any longer. Francis was dealing with Anton, and Maya had taken the deal. His son didn't need to be sitting around reading all day, or thinking he could be a Trojan any time soon. He would love for Matthew to take over from him one day. That day was not going to be today. He wanted the same things that Holly wanted for him.

A life away from Vale Valley, a chance for him to forge his own path and not have to wonder what the club thought.

Matthew was packing away the last of his clothes into a suitcase.

"Luna accepted the offer."

"I know. I asked her to."

"You love her, don't you, son?"

Matthew paused, and turned toward him. "Are you going to tell me that I'm too young to know what love is?"

"No. Everyone at any age should know what love is."

"Yeah, I love her, and I know she will never be mine."

"Why not?" Duke asked, moving into the room, and taking a seat on the bed. He loved his son so much. Matthew was one of the reasons why he waited so long to claim Holly as his own. He wanted to make sure she would be a good suit for Matthew.

"She will never trust me. I screwed her, and because I was a total asshole, I moved onto the next person, and then the next, and I screwed up."

Duke looked around the room. "I never thought you were the kind of kid that gave up. Look at the trophies, and remembering everything you've achieved in this world. You're not a quitter, and I didn't raise you to be one. You're a fighter, now act like the fighter that I know you are. You want Luna, go and get her."

"We go to different colleges."

"So, you think space would stop me going after Holly? I'd fight every single second of every single day to claim her, and to make her mine. If you want Luna, it wouldn't matter if she was in another country. You'd find a way to be with her. Don't you kids have that social media shit now? Years ago, you had to use pen and paper. Think about that. You've got it easy now." Duke stood up and made to leave the room.

"Thanks, Dad, for everything."

He turned to look at Matthew. "You're my son. I'll do whatever it takes to make you happy."

Chapter Eleven

Eliza was so nervous she was practically shaking in his arms. Brass took her hand and squeezed. She was nervous about this meeting at the Trojans MC clubhouse. Everyone was here, and her father hadn't gone away. According to Clinton he was trying to find a way to get the Trojans shut down. First he was going after the mechanic shop, which they had no choice but to close for inspection.

Their suppliers were also under investigation for where they got their alcohol and food. Mac had been closed because of his connection to the Trojans. Duke was pissed though because Holly and Mary's blog had been shut down as well.

All within forty-eight hours.

"They're going to hate me," she said.

"We don't hate you, Eliza," Duke said. He was sipping at his coffee while they waited for her father, Darcy, and Diaz to arrive. "You warned us about your father, and he can come after us. Unlike other companies and people, we have resources much like he has. We don't have the money, but we all have each other. Nothing is going to come between us. I can guarantee you that."

"I just don't want you going to—"

"Are you going to be Brass's old lady?" he asked.

"Yes."

"Then we're going to this much trouble. You belong to the club, and we protect what is ours. Don't worry about it. It's nice to have a few challenges in my life. It makes being Prez all that much more worth it."

"You're showing us you earned the patch?" Daisy said.

"You got it. The patch belongs to me, and don't

you boys forget it."

They all shared a laugh.

"I can't believe he went after a food blog. I mean seriously, we had just got together a competition for our readers, and like that poof, it's gone," Mary said. "Can I slap him?" she asked Pike.

"No, no slapping."

"What about a punch?" Holly asked. "Or I can kick him in the balls?"

"I'll get it all back for you," Duke said, kissing her hands.

She sighed. "It just pisses me off."

"In other good news, that contract you asked me to look at is legit," Clinton said. "They want you to sign a two book deal, and they will need you to do some touring when the book releases and some television appearances."

"We don't know if we want to take it," Holly said.

"That's crazy, why not?" Zoe asked.

"Because, we just like doing our little blog, and being at home, and sure our dream has always been to do with food, hasn't it?" Holly asked, looking toward Mary.

"Yeah. I'm in agreement with Holly. I really don't know if I want to do that level of commitment. I've got a baby coming, and then there's Starlight. I don't want to have to add travelling to the mix, and besides, television appearances? I don't know."

"It's your guys' decision," Duke said. "We will all support you."

Diaz entered the clubhouse, and he held his arms up. "I'm free and clear."

"Stop being an asshole," Raoul said, "Come on."

"I heard the good news, soon to be Daddy. You excited?"

"Yeah, I am."

Zoe rolled her eyes. "Will you boys ever grow up?"

"Nope. Uncle Diaz will always remain the cool one for the kids." Diaz winked, and made his way to his spot to the left of Duke.

Pike moved toward the right, and Brass wrapped his arms around Eliza. They heard the car pulling up, and he nuzzled Eliza's neck. She was so worried that this was going to turn bad. He was trying to offer her all of his support and love.

"I'm fine."

"You're not fine. I can feel how nervous you are."

"I've seen this happen so many times, Brass."

"Has anyone ever been as prepared as we are?" he asked.

"No."

"Then stop worrying. Have a little faith. We may not have money or the kind of power he has, but we have power here, and it's worth a lot more than his money." They had the power to ruin his reputation. Bishop was all about his reputation, and making sure everyone saw a perfect businessman, a thoroughly well-bred man. That was just an image that he put on. There was so much more fun to be had once you peeled away the bullshit.

Bishop and Darcy entered the clubhouse. Neither of them showed any sign of being nervous about this appearance.

"Step into my office," Duke said, kicking out the two chairs opposite him.

"I thought this was going to be a meeting," Bishop said.

"It is. You wanted to take on the Trojans, I thought it was only fair you see who you were dealing with. We're not all here today, but this is most of us. I'm Duke, and I'm the President of this club, and the man you've decided to declare war on."

Duke gave no sign of being pissed off.

Eliza's father went to speak.

"Oh, I know who you both are, so we don't need an introduction. Now. Who will I be conducting business with?"

"This is not a business discussion. I think we've made things quite plain. Give us my daughter, and we will make sure that your business remains intact."

Duke looked toward Eliza. "Do you want to go with them?"

She shook her head.

"I'm going to need you to speak up."

"No. I want to stay here."

Duke turned toward Clinton. "You witnessed that."

"I did."

"You see, Bishop, in Vale Valley, we own this town, and the people here are not afraid to stand up for the truth. You want to take us on, by all means go ahead. Eliza's staying here."

"Then I will kiss goodbye to your pathetic business. I will own everything within a week."

"And the entire world will know exactly what kind of man you are, and what you tried to get your young daughter to do," Duke said.

Bishop and Darcy had been about to stand, and they both turned around.

"Don't believe what lies my daughter says just for attention."

"Oh, these are not lies. You see, I did some digging when I noticed that Brass was falling for the prim and proper Eliza Bishop. I figured I should know more on the rich girl that was winning the heart of one of my men."

Diaz stepped forward. "It's not a pleasure to meet you." He handed the file to Duke.

"Diaz, be a sport, and get that laptop over there, and put this in it for me. Thank you." Duke flipped open the file. "Well, well, well." One by one, Duke placed photograph after photograph, along with medical DNA evidence sheets on the table. "Mr. Bishop, you have been a naughty, naughty boy. You have, as of two weeks ago, ten illegitimate children, with ten different women."

"What is the meaning of this?" Bishop asked.

"Play the tape, Diaz," Duke said.

Moans filled the room, and Brass chuckled as Eliza closed her eyes.

There on the laptop screen was her father, butt ass naked, screwing someone that was certainly not his wife.

"Oh fuck, yeah, fill me with your cock."

"You want that, slut. You want Daddy's cock."

"Ew!" Eliza said, then covered her ears.

Bishop went to Diaz, and Raoul held him back.

"We're not done. Skip to the next video."

This time it showed Darcy with a man, fucking.

"As you can see, gentlemen, it doesn't take money to get this kind of evidence. And you would also be pleased to know that of those ten children, every single one of them would be more than happy to do a television interview about the father that abandoned them. Imagine that. All those kids, some forced to grow up in poverty because you decided not to claim them. Three of them ended up in foster homes." This time Duke stood up. "I do my homework. You come after anyone of this club, and I will come after you."

"What do you want?" Bishop asked.

"You to leave town and forget about Eliza unless it's for a nice big family reunion. You stay the fuck away from my business, and if you even breathe a word of any shit about the Trojan name, Eliza Bishop, or Diaz, or fucking Vale Valley, then every single piece of this shit will go public!"

"How do I know that you wouldn't do it now?"

"I've had this stuff in my possession for weeks. I have no use for it. I guess it's what we'd like to call a business deal, Mr. Bishop."

"Did Duke win?" Eliza asked, whispering to him.

"Holy fuck did he win. Your father is a horn dog. He could even pass as a Trojan they've got that much shit on him."

"That's gross. I can't even unsee that stuff."

"Consider this a deal."

Bishop and Darcy didn't stick around. They left, and Brass saw the smile on Eliza's face. He cupped her cheek, stroking his thumb across her pale flesh. "Why are you so happy?"

"I never thought I could be this happy to see them leave, but I am. I'm finally free."

"Does this mean you don't want to be my old lady?" he asked.

She slapped his chest. "I'm going to be your old lady now without fear. I was always worried that they would come, and they would try to ruin what you and I have." This time she cupped his cheek. "I love you, Brass. I love you more than anything in the world."

"Well you better remember this then because I'm going to piss you off. I'm going to make you crazy so that you'll want to chase after me with a skillet."

She burst out laughing.

He caught her up toward him, slamming his lips down on hers.

Only at the sound of Duke clearing his throat did he let her go.

"I expect you to take Brass as your old man. I

look forward to having you part of our team." Duke shook her hand, and Brass knew that he'd made the right decision. For himself, for the love of the club. For everything.

****

The following week flew by. Bishop and Darcy left town, and the moment they were gone, Eliza felt that she could breathe a lot easier. It was next to impossible to think with either of them breathing down her neck. From the moment she'd seen Darcy at her front door, she had been so tense, and unable to think or focus on anything.

"Are you ready for this evening?" Holly asked.

They both had trolleys and were gathering up food for the barbeque. "I'm nervous, but I want to do this for Brass. It's important to both of us, and he made sacrifices for me. I think it's only fair that I do the same with him." She loaded her trolley with several cans of tomatoes while Holly took care of the beans. Bell, Holly's little girl, was sitting in one of the trolleys with a toy.

"Did you hear that Zoe is in fact pregnant?"

"No, I didn't. I know she did the test and it came in positive, but she doesn't trust tests, does she?" Eliza asked.

"No. She doesn't. One of them got her hopes up only to learn that nothing was there. They went to the doctor, and ta-da, they are pregnant. I'm so excited. We're going to need to throw a celebration party as well as a baby shower. I love children." Holly pressed a kiss to Bell's cheek, and then blew a raspberry. Bell chuckled.

"You're a good mother."

"I try. Matthew is back at college now, and that is always a tough one. I don't like him being away from home."

"You've been a good mom to him. Was that

weird? You're not that much older than him, right."

Holly shrugged. "He's a kid, and his mother was a bitch. She neglected him, and a lot worse stuff, believe me. Duke said it helped that Matthew had a crush on me. I don't think that is true. I think I was just the first woman to actually talk to him, you know. Sit down and find out what was wrong with him."

They moved to the fridges, and both started to load up on the cheese.

"Where is his mom?" Eliza asked.

Holly stood. "I don't know. Somewhere. We've not heard from her, and Matthew's good. So, what are you going to wear?"

Clearly, Matthew's mother was a sore subject. "I don't know. Do you think I should wear something sexy?"

Holly covered Bell's ears. "You're going to have sex. Of course you're going to want to look sexy." She blew another raspberry on Bell's cheeks and lowered her hands.

This was not a conversation for tender ears.

"How is Maya?" Eliza asked.

Holly sighed. "Again, this is a hard one. She's my sister, half-sister, whatever you want to call her. I don't know what to say to her. It seems really weird right now. I've not been able to talk to my mom and Russ. I can't even call Russ 'Dad' anymore. It's all messed up."

"You'll get there. It's understandable you feeling a little lost. I've learned I've got brothers and sisters everywhere. They will all probably hate me because I got to live with my dad."

"I wonder if Maya hates me. I bet she does. I would hate me as well. I live in Vale Valley, the life I've lived just from the pictures alone shows I had a great one. I'm married to the love of my life, got kids, and I'm living the dream. She was raped and tortured. Spent most of her life miserable, and I don't know what to say to her."

"Maybe you could start with, 'how are you getting on? I'm Holly and I'm as nervous as you'?" Eliza tried to offer suggestions.

"I try. When I see her I have the best of intentions, but then I just freeze up and walk away. She probably thinks that I hate her, and I don't. I'm just confused, and trying to make my way in the world like everyone else."

"You really need to talk to her though. It's important that you do."

"Yeah, I do. I'll do it. I will do it. Tonight at the bonfire. Before or after your old lady thing, I'll talk to her."

"I'd do it before. My old lady thing is not happening until late, really, really late."

Holly laughed. "Let's hope you don't get a taste for being watched. You'll be trying to get someone to watch you then."

Eliza stuck her tongue out, and then burst out laughing. It was fun having some time with the girls.

After they got all the good, Holly dropped her off back at home, and she spent the rest of the afternoon wondering what the hell to wear.

It wasn't a sex party, and it was warm now. Should she wear jeans? He was going to be taking them off her. Could she risk a skirt?

Wow, so many decisions.

****

After storing everything in the pantry, Holly made her way into the kitchen to find Maya sitting at the table doing something in a book. She stared at her for a few seconds until Maya looked up at her. Holly froze up, and being a complete coward, she turned around and went straight into the pantry.

Staring at the abundant shelves filled with food, she gripped the pole of one of the shelves, and rested her head against it. "You can do this. It's not hard to do. Just talk to her, and you'll be fine."

She took a deep breath, and made her way into the kitchen to find Maya packing up.

"Wait, where are you going?" Holly asked.

Maya looked up, and Holly's stomach knotted. "I know you're uncomfortable being around me. I'll go study outside. It's no big deal."

"No, wait."

Maya stopped by the door.

"I'm not uncomfortable around you. At least not in the way you think." Maya turned toward her, and Holly took a seat at the table. Her hands were shaking. She was so nervous. This was completely unlike her. "Please, sit with me. I would like it if you would. I'm not all bad. I promise. Just a bit weird, that is all."

Slowly, Maya sat down opposite her.

Holly took a deep breath. "I … I'm not uncomfortable with you. It's hard. You knew our real father, and for the longest time I didn't even know I had another father."

"I know. You didn't miss much. Our dad was a monster."

"This is what I mean. I've had a really good life, Maya."

"You think I hate you?"

"Yeah, I do."

"I don't hate you, Holly. I never have. I knew about you, and he always talked about you. I hoped that you were nothing like him, and you aren't. It means that I have hope."

"You're nothing like that horrible man, or like Francis."

Maya smiled. "That's good to know, I think."

"I want us to get to know each other. Not just as sisters but as friends. I want to be there for you. I always wanted a sister or a brother."

"I would really like that."

Holly stood, and opened her arms. "Then hug me. Come on, bring it on, give me a hug."

Maya got to her feet, and then wrapped her arms around Holly. As she closed her eyes, the knots in her stomach faded. She had a sister, and she was going to work on that.

Chapter Twelve

"You look beautiful," Brass said.

She had settled on a pair of jeans and a crop top shirt with Brass's leather jacket. He had walked in right in the middle of her little temper tantrum. She had refused to go, and when he had told her she had no choice, she had made him pick her clothes.

"Of course you think that. You picked everything."

He rolled his eyes. "Anyone ever tell you that you can be an annoying pain in the ass?" he asked.

She sighed. "I feel stupid. I know why we're here."

"We're here to have fun, to mingle, eat really good food."

"Have sex. Don't forget that last part."

"You are not the first, and you will not be the last with this, babe." He pressed a kiss to her temple. "Relax, otherwise you're going to spoil it for yourself."

The moment they entered the clubhouse parking lot, Holly rushed toward her, and pulled her away. Brass went for a beer, and toward the barbeque area. The coals were already being prepared on the burning fire.

"Your woman has made a friend out of Holly," Duke said, moving toward him.

"She has?"

"Yeah. They went shopping earlier, and Eliza convinced her to talk with Maya. Holly listened, and now they are going to work on being close."

"I'm pleased. Not just for my girl but for Holly and Maya." He had seen the ghosts in the younger girl's eyes. It was hard to ignore that kind of emotion, and now it was even more so.

Sipping at his beer, he looked around the

clubhouse. "Everyone is here?"

"Knuckles and Beth are still on their honeymoon. Daisy and Maria have taken their kid for a mini vacation. All is good though," Duke said. "Matthew got back to campus safely. Luna is in her college. I've got a feeling I'll be seeing more of that girl in a few years."

"She may leave Vale Valley," Brass said.

"Nah, Vale Valley, it's in your blood. You can't ignore the calling of your town, and this place has a lot to offer."

"I wonder which brother will be next to follow this path."

Duke glanced around. "Pie could be next. He's too damn cocky. Actually, I want him to fall next. It'll teach that fucker a lesson in love."

Brass burst out laughing. "Yeah, I could see that."

"It could be anyone. This isn't a game though. We will see what happens."

"To the Trojans," Brass said.

"To the Trojans," Duke said.

"Actually, we should be congratulating Duke on kicking everyone's ass," Pike said. "I think you turned Diaz on as well. You killed it with Bishop and that other fucker."

"I didn't even need to use my fists either. That's a good thing. Holly hates it when I get bloody."

"Speaking of old ladies. Eliza was pretty nervous so I'm going to go and keep her company." Brass made his way toward the group of women. Wrapping his arms around Eliza, he pulled her close. Pressing his lips against her neck, he breathed in her scent. "Hey, baby. You're still here."

"I'm still here. I think Holly's under instructions to keep me close."

"I'm not. I'm just under instructions to make sure

you're happy." Holly winked.

"They're going to start up some food. Let's dance."

The music was softly playing, and Brass pulled her into his arms. He didn't care that they were the only ones that were dancing. He was just thrilled to have her in his arms.

"Are you okay?" he asked.

"Yeah, I'm fine. I'm happy. Thank you so much for everything, Brass."

"I love you, babe. There is nothing to thank me for. I will do everything for you, in a heartbeat."

"That is why I love you." She rested her head against his chest, and he wrapped his arms around her.

After their dance, Duke announced that some food was ready, so Brass did his best trying to distract Eliza. There was food. More slow dancing, and a lot of loving. The night wore on, and some of the club left to go home, while others made their way inside.

When there was no more time to wait, Brass took her hand and led her inside.

The lights were down low, and the music was soft.

The men that were staying were already there, and the door was shut.

"This is it?" she asked.

"This is it. Tonight, you're all mine, Eliza. No turning back, no running away. You will belong to me."

"I'm not going anywhere." She cupped his face and pressed her lips to his. He felt the tremors in her body. She was nervous but was doing this for them, for the club.

Slamming his lips down on hers, he moved her back, going toward the pool table. Chip and Pie had been playing a game of pool. Both brothers moved away, taking their cues with them.

The brothers' gazes were on them, and he felt their stares in the back of his neck, all around him.

Brass had participated in the club whores, and watched a few of the old ladies. He had been envious then, and now he knew what it was all about.

"No one will see you," he said. Eliza belonged to him. Her pussy, ass, mouth, tits, every single part of her belonged to him, and he didn't like sharing.

"Please," she said, moaning his name.

Lifting her up, he placed her down on the pool table, needing her eyes on him. She wouldn't be able to focus on anything else if he took her a different way. Brass wanted her gaze on him so that she knew who was fucking her, who was claiming her, and who was owning her.

Opening her jeans, he eased them down to her knees, and only removed one leg. The jacket he wore hid her thigh from sight. This was about his woman's comfort as much as the club. He had spoken to Duke to make sure he could give her as much privacy while also claiming her.

Tearing her panties off her body, he pocketed them as well. Pulling down his zipper, his cock sprang free, and he slowly eased inside her body. Her pussy was soaking wet, squeezing him with each inch that he slid inside her. She was still so incredibly tight.

"Brass!" She cried out his name, and he relished the sounds, knowing there was never going to be any other woman quite like her. Eliza belonged to him just as he belonged to her.

"I love you, baby." He slammed ever single inch of his dick inside her, relishing the pulse of her cunt. Keeping his gaze on her, he waited for her to get accustomed to his dick, and only when she started to wriggle did he begin to fuck her. Plunging in and out of her, he took his time, making love to her, drawing out her cries, and need for him and the entire room to hear.

Everything faded into the background, and he made love to her. Reaching between them, he stroked her clit, hearing the sounds of her cries as she catapulted over the edge into orgasm.

Brass wasn't going to last long, and he filled her pussy with his spunk, knowing that in the eyes of the Trojans, his woman would be forever looked after.

****

Being made love to in a roomful of men was erotic, it was alluring, and it was entirely embarrassing. Eliza didn't know if she made a lot of noise or if anyone heard her. Either way, it was over, and she was now Brass's old lady. She was even going to get some ink as well. She had seen Holly's ink across her back. It was black thorns, and below was Duke's name. Eliza wanted Brass's name inked on her skin.

The sun was up, and it was a bright new day. She was outside, picking up the last of the bottles, and throwing them in the recycle can.

"You look chipper this morning," Holly said, moving out to join her.

"I am. I'm in a world of bliss."

"You enjoyed it, didn't you?" Holly asked.

Her cheeks heated. "I did enjoy it a little bit. I'm not going to lie. You're up early."

"Yeah. My mom's dropping the kids off to Mary's and I'll pick them up later. I've asked her and Russ here, and I wanted to talk to them. You know, I talked with Maya, and we're going to get close. I think it's time I made up with my parents. Russ may not be my biological dad, but he's still my dad, if that makes any sense at all."

Eliza giggled. "It does make sense. I'm so pleased."

Just then a car pulled into the parking lot, and Eliza saw it was Russ and Sheila. "They're here." Holly gave her a hug, and Eliza went back to picking up the last of the bottles. There had to be a way of making this an easier clean up. She was humming to herself when she heard the first shout.

Turning toward the sound she saw a man, a really scared, almost beastly looking man. He had two guns in his hands. Both of them were pointed at Russ and Sheila.

Her heart began to pound, and she looked toward the clubhouse door.

"What's it going to be, Holly? Your mommy or your daddy?" the man asked.

"Put the damn gun down," Russ said.

"You think I didn't know what kind of deal you made. You think you could silence me. I gave you a fucking choice, Holly, and now it's going to happen. Your mother or your father!"

Duke, Brass, Maya, and several of the brothers made their way outside. They had spotted the guns, and had their own raised.

"Anton, what the fuck are you doing?" Duke asked.

"You think because you went to my dad that all was done? I gave you an ultimatum. Sheila or Russ."

"Anton, you don't want to do this," Sheila said.

"I don't. I would have great satisfaction of ending the fucking both of you, but as it is, you don't mess with the Trojans. Even the Abelli have a respect for them right now, because of you." Anton was now looking at Duke. "Get Daddy on the phone. I don't care. I'm done."

Guns went off, and Eliza screamed at the same time as Holly. She was pushed to the ground, and when she looked up, she saw that Brass was on top of her.

"No," Holly said, screaming.

Getting to her feet with Brass surrounding her, Eliza took in the sight before her. Sheila was down, and Holly was over her. There was also no sign of Russ.

Holly was pressing against Sheila's chest, and sobbing.

Anton was tackled to the ground, and Duke was by his woman's side.

Eliza saw the blood.

"Call an ambulance!" Holly screamed, and Pike was already on it, putting a call through.

"This is bad," Chip said from the other side of the car.

Brass left her, and she watched as Sheila and Russ were worked on by the club, trying to keep them alive. Anton was escorted into the clubhouse, and he also had a gunshot wound.

Eliza saw that Maya was crouched on the floor, and she went straight to her.

"Everything is going to be messed up," Maya said. "I'm cursed. I hurt everything."

She wrapped her arms around Maya, and held her close. "You're not cursed. This was that asshole's fault. Not yours."

The sirens for the ambulances filled the air, and for the next twenty minutes, everything went to shit. Brass moved toward her covered in blood.

Landon took Maya and headed back into the clubhouse.

"Russ didn't make it. He's dead."

"No." She looked toward Holly, who was trying to help the ambulance crew get her mother on the stretcher.

"It doesn't look good for Sheila."

"What does this mean?" Eliza asked.

"We've got Anton. This is all on Duke again. Anton came after one of our own. If Sheila dies, I don't know what will happen. He'll do anything for Holly. If she wants the whole of Abelli gone, then we will go and kill every single one of them."

She nodded.

"Are you okay, baby?" Brass looked worried.

"I'm fine. I'll go and help. I'm here, Brass. I'm not going anywhere." She was in this for the long haul. They were staying together.

****

Duke wrapped his arms around Holly as she curled up in the chair. His heart was breaking for her. He had known she was planning to spend time with both Sheila and Russ.

"Any news?" Chip asked.

"Nothing yet. She's in surgery."

Holly sobbed.

Chip took a step toward him, and handed him a note.

Francis is on his way.

He nodded. He would deal with Francis when the time was right. For now, his woman needed him.

Kissing her temple, he closed his eyes, knowing that this was going to be hard for her. It didn't look good. He had seen the doubt on the paramedic's face when trying to deal with Sheila.

Pie came into the waiting room, and sat down next to them. Next were Brass and Eliza. Pike was at the clubhouse keeping an eye on Anton. Mary was taking care of his kids.

The minutes passed that soon turned into an hour. Two hours. Three hours.

Finally a doctor came out, and just from looking

at his face, Duke knew the truth.

Sheila was gone.

****

Later that night Duke stood inside the basement of the Trojans MC. The club whores were gone, and all that remained were his close brothers. The monster who had destroyed his woman sat on a chair, tied up.

"She's dead, isn't she?" Anton asked, laughing. "I knew I'd gotten to her finally. It's about time someone put that fucking bitch in the ground."

Duke said nothing, and simply stared at the man that he hated more than anything. "You made my girl cry."

"Her mother was a fucking whore, and she deserved it. I told you to pick one. You didn't. You went behind my fucking back to my father. Do you really think I wouldn't find out?"

"I didn't give a fuck. You're not the head of the Abelli. You're a disgrace."

Anton stopped laughing. "You can't kill me."

"I can't?"

"To kill me would incite a war."

Duke held his arms open. "You started this. You see, I had an agreement with the real head of the Abelli family. Maya stays quiet, Francis gets to see his grandkids, and you stayed away from us. Any deal we had fucking ended the moment you put a bullet in Russ and Sheila." He grabbed the nearest blade and slammed it into Anton's thigh. Duke relished the screams that poured from his throat. "Give it to me, Anton. Your ass is all mine. You will not be leaving this basement alive."

He pulled the blade out, and slowly thrust it into Anton's shoulder. There was no emotion inside him. All he could hear was Holly's screams as her parents were taken from her. There was no remorse in this asshole, and anyone who made Holly cry, got hurt.

Pulling the blade out of the shoulder, Duke landed blow after blow against the man's fucked up face.

Duke didn't know how much time had passed, and he didn't care. By the time Francis came in, Anton was hanging on by a thread.

"I'm so sorry. How is Holly?" Francis asked.

Holding the blade against Anton's throat, Duke stared at the man who he had trusted. "She screamed, Francis. She begged for their lives, and this fucker still pulled the trigger."

"I'm sorry, but this is not the way."

"He will not be leaving my clubhouse alive."

Francis dropped his hand. "Do not do this. Do not start a war that you cannot win."

"A war? You think this is going to start a war?" Duke stared at Francis. "You promised me, Francis *Abelli*." He made sure the Abelli name was filled with disgust, which was exactly how he felt. He pointed the blade at Francis. "You promised me Sheila and Russ would be safe. You gave me your word."

"Duke, this is not the way. A war with me will not work."

Duke burst out laughing. "I'll win. You betrayed me."

"I did no such thing."

"You promised me that Sheila and Russ would be safe. Your word. You said that you'll deal with Anton. Yet he came to my clubhouse, and shot two of my people. You declared war on me."

"He's my oldest son. I beg you. Whatever you want, I will grant it."

"I will let Anton go free. I will let him walk out of here right now."

"Thank you."

"But the Abelli name will end. I already have it in my power to declare war on you, Francis Abelli. Anton walks out of here, and every single enemy, every single ally will know that Abelli means shit!"

Duke stared at him.

"You don't know everyone," Francis said, giving away his fear by turning pale.

"I don't? Do you even know the relevance of why we're called the Trojans?" He waited a few seconds. "Men like you don't see us coming. We move in, and we find out your weaknesses. We find them, exploit them, and turn that shit against them. All you had to do was keep Anton in check. Keep him away from my town. You didn't do that. You failed, and I have all the evidence I need to make it go public." He stood and walked toward the television, playing the security footage that showed Anton acting against his father. "Were those your orders? Did the great Francis Abelli keep his little boy in check? Tell me, Francis. Is this what a deal means with you?" Duke saw he was getting to Francis. A powerful man was only so powerful if he kept to his word, and those around him, trusted him. "I wonder what the great *Abelli* name would be like once I start." Duke shrugged. "Either way, I don't end him, then you won't have to worry about a sixteen year old girl telling tales."

"You'd turn rat?" Francis asked.

"Not on my club." Duke burst out laughing. "There is nothing binding me or my club to you. That," he pointed at the television, "binds you to murder. I can find everything I need. Now, do you want to take him? Your precious oldest son!" He moved behind Anton, digging his fingers into Anton's arm. "Tick-tock."

He stared at Francis knowing either option wasn't the best. Lose a son, or lose his entire name. Duke would make sure Abelli was destroyed, and he would do it slowly, bit by bit.

"Dad," Anton said, trying to speak. The word was easy to make out, even though it was hurting Anton to say a single word. Duke pressed the blade against Anton's throat.

Francis fisted his hands. "I see no reason for this to go any further, and in fact, you would be doing me a service."

"Mom, no, Mom."

Holly's screams rang through his head. They would stay with him until the day he died. Pulling the blade away from Anton's throat, he watched as Francis tensed up. In the next second, Duke pierced Anton's throat, and held him still as Francis watched. Duke stared at Francis as Anton's life ended.

Releasing Anton's dead body, he watched as it slumped forward. Holding the knife he approached Francis. Holding out the blade, he placed it in Francis's hands. "I want you out of my fucking town, and if anyone comes to my town in any association of Abelli, I will kill every single one of you. You think you're a monster?" Duke moved in closer. "You don't know who you're fucking dealing with." Duke had done his fair share of evil, and he wasn't afraid to keep doing it again. "Back off, or Abelli will be a name no one remembers."

Dropping the bloodied blade into his hand, Duke walked away. His job was done.

****

Later that night, Duke made his way home to where his girl was. Holly was curled up in bed, sobbing.

"Anton's gone," he said.

"Good. He's a monster."

Duke had already washed and changed out of his clothes. "I will declare war on Abelli, babe. Tell me what you want me to do and I'll do it."

Holly sniffled. "You'd risk the club for me."

"I would do anything to make you happy. The club, they will follow me, and I will kill every last Abelli. Just tell me what you want."

She didn't say anything for the longest time. Duke wasn't joking. Francis wouldn't make it out of Vale Valley alive. All she had to do was give him the word.

"Hold me, Duke. Just hold me."

Chapter Thirteen

Francis Abelli left town, and no one heard from him. Knuckles returned home with Beth to two funerals. Brass held Eliza's hand as they stood by Russ and Sheila's graveside. Even Matthew had returned to say his goodbyes.

No one could really believe it. Brass couldn't grasp that he was never going to see Russ's ugly face or Sheila's smiling one. It was an end of an era with the two gone. He didn't even want to admit that they were gone. Their blood had been on his hands.

Glancing over at Holly, he saw she was struggling to keep it together. Everyone was dressed in black.

He squeezed Eliza's hand, trying to offer her comfort. She was giving him more comfort though.

"I'm here," she said, whispering the words to him.

The service ended, and each of them threw roses onto the coffins. Duke held onto Holly tightly. Mary, Matthew, and Pike were helping with the kids during this time.

"I can't believe he's gone," Knuckles said, coming to stand beside him.

"I know. It happened so fast."

"I know what happened. Duke told me." Knuckles turned to Eliza. "Congratulations. It's good news for the two of you."

"Thank you," Eliza said.

This wasn't the time for congratulations.

"We better be heading back."

The whole of Vale Valley had turned out for Russ and Sheila's send off. They may not have known it alive, but they had touched the hearts of the entire town. The reception had to be held in the town square there were so many people.

They walked toward the town square along with everyone else. Eliza rested her head against his chest.

"I'm so sorry you lost someone you loved," she said.

"He was part of the club. Russ was a good guy. Had bad methods at times but he was a good guy."

"I know."

The walk didn't take that long. Brass grabbed himself a beer and Eliza a glass of wine.

They stood with Leanna and Crazy talking about the service when Pie and Chip joined them.

"Who is that woman?" Chip asked.

"I saw her fucking first," Pie said.

"Seriously, this is a fucking funeral and you're looking at the ass available?" Brass asked.

"Look, it's sad, but Russ wouldn't blame us. She's fucking hot." Chip pointed toward Duke and Holly.

Crazy started laughing. "You two don't have a chance with her. She's a nurse, and her name is Kasey. She has too much class for the two of you."

Brass saw the look on Pie's and Chip's faces. They were both going to compete to prove Crazy wrong.

The service was long, and it was tiring. Brass hated every second of it, so by the time he got back to his own place with Eliza he was more than happy. She kicked off her heels, as he pushed his shoes off his feet. "That was fucking exhausting," he said.

"You should be nice. It was hard on everyone," she said.

"I know. I hate funerals. I always have."

"I don't think anyone is supposed to enjoy it. Funerals are all supposed to suck." She snuggled in against him on their sofa.

Brass held his woman and closed his eyes, basking in her scent. "It's the loss that I can't handle.

Funerals are supposed to be about celebrating the person's life."

"They're great for people who have lived their entire life, Brass. This was about more than the loss of life. It was taken. They were murdered."

"I know." He kissed the top of her head, and rummaged in his pocket. "It also spoilt my plans. I know I sound heartless, but I planned everything."

"Planned what?" she asked.

He pulled out the velvet box. "I was kind of hoping you'd be my wife, and do me the honor of marrying me."

She had frozen beside him. "You were going to propose?"

"Yeah. I was going to take you for a romantic meal, candles, nice words, and all the shit. I was hoping to impress you, and if that didn't work I'd have fucked you into oblivion."

Eliza giggled. "You're still not good with words, are you?"

"I'm hoping my actions speak a lot louder than my words."

She tilted her head back to look at him.

"Are you going to put me out of my misery?" he asked.

"I don't know. I think I like you kind of sweating over what my answer is going to be."

He slammed his lips down on hers, and held her close, leaving her breathless. He wasn't going to take no for an answer. "Tell me, baby."

She opened her eyes, which had closed as he kissed her. Cupping his cheek, she ran her thumb across his lip. "I love you, Brass. Yes. A million and one times yes."

That day was one of the worst of his life, but Eliza

made it all so worth it by giving herself to him. He would make her as happy as she made him.

Epilogue

Two years later

"What do you think?" Brass asked.

"That Duke has way too much land." Eliza placed her hands behind her back, and stared out across the acres of land. There was so much of it, and Duke had decided to expand, building several houses closer to his.

Brass moved up behind his woman, nuzzling her neck and placing his hands on her very heavy stomach. "I want to put an offer on a place."

"What's wrong with our apartment?" she asked.

"One of the rooms is your office, which you need as a bestselling author, and well, we need a room for these guys." He was having twins. After two years together, a year and a half of wedded bliss, they were weeks away from being parents. Brass loved Eliza more every single day. She had come along way, and since her family had stopped having anything to do with her, she had flourished in ways that made him so proud.

She was so beautiful, and she had earned the respect of the club as his old lady. Standing by his side, by Holly's side, everyone had found out how strong she was.

"Twins. You never warned me that you had multiple kids in your family," she said.

"I didn't know. You're avoiding the question. Two little terrors are going to need a room to sleep, and a place to make mischief. My apartment is not big enough, and neither is the clubhouse. You know you love it out here. When we visit Duke and Holly, you always look at peace."

She spun around in his arms. "I don't want us to be struggling for money," she said.

"You won't be. I'm giving Brass, and any of the

club brothers a discount," Duke said, coming to stand with them. "You'll have your privacy. I know Mary and Pike are taking the house just behind mine, and then this will be your plot." Duke moved across the fields. Standing behind Eliza, he guided her in the same direction. "Think about it, Eliza. Here you could have a nice big kitchen overlooking our yard. The kids can mingle. We can leave everything open or you can have a fence. I don't mind. We're all a family. You've got room for an office, sitting room, dining room, and you'll be close."

Brass knew it was what she always wanted. She had spoken to him many times over the past three months about this plot of land. After the tenth time, he had taken the hint, and talked to Duke finally securing this plot.

Eliza spun around in his arms. "You really do listen."

"Actions, baby. This is one of those moments."

She pressed her lips against his, giggling.

"Do you want it?" he asked.

"Do you?"

"I want what you do."

"I would love it."

He turned to Duke. "I'll take it."

"Good. I already got the builders ready to come out. It will take some time, but you can always keep progress on the house."

Duke left them alone, and Brass held his woman. "How are you doing?" he asked.

"My ankles are hurting, and so is my back. Our sons do not like sitting down."

"They are going to make life interesting for us," Brass said.

"For me, it already is." She sank her fingers into his hair, holding him close.

He never thought it was possible to love someone this fiercely. Eliza was his soul mate, the other half of him, and he would do anything for her. Even when she was squeezing the life out of his hand a few weeks later. She gave birth to their two little terrors. She had given him a family, and he had given her love. Nothing could be better in his world.

The End

www.samcrescent.wordpress.com

SAM CRESCENT

EVERNIGHT PUBLISHING ®

www.evernightpublishing.com